Marisa

Peter Cowlam

Published by CentreHouse Press 2006

www.centrehousepress.co.uk

Copyright © 2006, Peter Cowlam

ISBN 1-902086-03-1
ISBN 978-1-902086-03-3

Printed and bound by BookSurge, LLC
an Amazon.com company

inquiries@centrehousepress.co.uk

For Jack Kendrick

1

MY AUTUMNS ARE always like this: that almost forgotten suburb of my birth, just a blur of dampish twilit streets for the last twenty-five Octobers, shifts into focus suddenly — a mental or concrete atmosphere infallibly timed to undermine my walk from the station to my office. There is a gust of burnished orange leaves, a freight that having left the trees, and swirling across the streets and squares, marks the anniversary of one of those tedious family dramas, which I'd rather not dredge up. In the breeze of that one instant I consider a simple call to my secretary, cancelling all appointments, a park bench appealing to me more, where having turned up my collar the hum of business melts away, bringing time, at last, to reflect.

That decision is never made. Invariably, at a few minutes to nine, the glassy motif etched in the atrium door seals my world of moving capital from the cold exhilarating eddies outside. A marble-faced security man, paid to scrutinise a bank of TV screens, signals our exclusive fraternity — I am emperor, and this is my empire — and with usual deliberation avoids my second glance.

These are delicate times, I say, and insist on showing ID. I summon a lift, and wait there in the foyer, just watching for its clock to run down. Then strike those two demotic notes of its chime, so that now, as I cross hands several times over my document case, I leave all sentiment to the bluster outside, the whole day before me measured in a womb of padded walls, as I rise to the heights of my penthouse. Already a dozen overseas investors have wished me good morning, leaving messages, all wanting me to phone.

On this particular Monday, shaking off those snares of my past wasn't quite as straightforward. Gladys, as usual ironic, had dusted Father's bust, a bronze head and shoulders done shamelessly Churchillian-style, and was waiting for me aimlessly as our coffee strained through its filter. I sat down, my back to the window, still unbuttoning my coat. I switched on my computer. I bathed my cheeks in the hues that filled its screen.

Then, having hung my coat, I began my day with the first of my monthly reports — shares, mortgages, insurance. There was one list I always insisted on, because it plotted, according to turnover, small companies seeking new investments. I scrolled through it, checking any names I hadn't seen before, then backtracked suddenly, to confirm an address I knew, an old rambling house called (curiously) Aitkin Aspires, a place tucked away behind a terrace of small business properties and private dwellings edging Ealing Common. Its owner was Marisa Rae, or rather still Marisa Rae — there after a lifetime aeon of twenty-five years.

2

IN THOSE DAYS of course my father — Bruce Senior — was very much alive, and not yet thinking of busts, portraits, or any other guarantee of his posterity. His was the evangelising principle. He insisted on the material transformation of honest hard work — in this case his, and later mine — to a stouter fabric for the firm he ran. This he had built himself from a handful of shares he'd inherited young, mostly blue chip, though one or two were genuinely exotic. However, not all augured well for the succession he had in mind. I was not an attentive student, and scraped only a lower second in the business degree I half-heartedly entered into — that after the expense of a private, and often futile education (one of those cool observations I hear echo even now). I enjoyed the college bars and unwadded most of my cash there, and lavished it not only on myself. I got involved backstage with theatre productions (a *Royal Hunt of the Sun* is memorable still), though never quite had the courage to audition for parts, tempted as I often was. Nights I played draw poker in only my swim shorts and sucking a cigar, till dawn and its twitters made bed a better prospect. That particular gamble I found cut short when an inflamed appendix brought with it unexpected revelations. There was only one book to hand, while I recovered after surgery, and that was a delve into the complex dilemmas faced by the sixth Dalai Lama. It's a cliché now, in a world of colliding cultures, that here was my foil for the values of Western society – a tonnage I had sometimes groaned under, but so far taken for granted. The dust cover showed someone supposedly the great man himself, with members of his retinue, all in various spiritual poses, pictured on the timber deck of an oriental pavilion. So there *were* other things apart from an English middle-class.

Bruce Senior's first decree, as I entered the family firm, debarred me, at least for the time being, from an office or staff of my own, most of whom – men and women in their thirties – would resent my being their boss, understandably. One of our portfolios, not exactly essential to the business, was control of a pension fund he'd picked up cheap in the early 1970s. Among its modest list, a significant number lived as expatriates. For example there was one ancient couple in Vienna. In another, a former highway engineer had stayed on with the much younger bride he'd found in Bogata. A lot had ventured east, either to Hong Kong or Singapore – or farther, to Perth, Melbourne, Sydney – though the majority choice was the cities, plains and holiday resorts dotting the Iberian peninsula. One perennial question these happy weatherworn people always faced was how to receive their pay – in pounds sterling or their local currency. Whole mornings I spent pulling on hats and slacks and sunblocks, getting to grips, in the slant of my mirror, with the opening patter my first commission came with: 'You know most if they make a choice make a wrong choice.' The firm wouldn't run to flights and hotel bills in either South America or anywhere near the Pacific rim, and so I settled on a flying visit to half a dozen clients who'd made their lives in Spain.

My youth and natural good temper were the right bag of tools in selling other financial products as I combed their affairs, a ploy so successful, surprisingly, that the lowlands of Andalusia hosted my return often enough to postpone, indefinitely, a redistribution of desk space back at the London office. However, not all my clients had settled for an outdoor life testing the loungers lining the Mediterranean shores. One of my ex-Home Counties bankers had invested in the muscat grape, a man intimate with kosher produce and the demands of all kinds of Jewish celebrations. In the days of my first portfolio he exported to synagogues practically everywhere, his product a fortified wine – red and too sweet for my taste – by whose appellation its origin was better known – i.e., Málaga. Málaga City he wouldn't ever take me to, though Granada and Cádiz he did. From the latter my albums quickly filled with snaps of its salt ponds, marshy lagoons, the orchards, vineyards, olive groves, the cork trees up in the mountains, and endlessly the views I never quite tired of, up and down the branch line from Seville to Algeciras.

My banker-turned-entrepreneur heartily apprised me of all his professional insight into the variety of grape he used in his manufacturing process, describing with aplomb the sun-dry technique that concentrated its sweetness. This was a cheery exchange that always put him in good, expansive mood. One gesture alone took in all the sierras, then with his lopsided smile he drove me in his Jeep to the caves of El Romeral, from where my many postcards home catalogued the entire holiday expanse. It seemed important enough that once back in the leafy greys of Ealing I enrolled for an adult course in conversational Spanish — a class of twenty-odd, run by a thinly moustached Isabel McFadden (or MacFard — her name I can't fully recall). By lesson two I had already exchanged a first thoughtless desk for a spare I had noted much nearer to Marisa's, who remained within herself, and as a student was very conscientious. Her flesh was unblemished ivory, and her hair was flame.

I never quite engineered the right moment to engage her socially, and so left the whole thing to chance, which duly arrived one blustery evening when Isabel paired us for fluency practice (these the stupendous edicts of fate). That threw us together in a stutter of awkward conversation, mine the part of hopeful Anglo-Spanish suitor, and both with a great capacity for lung cancer:

'Buenas tardes, señorita. ¿Habla Vd. español?'

'No muy bien, señor…señor…'

'The name's Bruce.'

'¡Español!' (a shrieking McFadden).

'Perdón. Me llamo Bruce. ¿Cómo se llama?'

'Me llamo Marisa.'

'Marisa. ¿Y de dónde eres?'

'Soy de west London, Bruce.'

'As I am too.'

'¡Bruce!'

'Perdón, Isabel. ¿Vd. fuma, Marisa?'

'Con mucho gusto. Vd. es muy amable. ¿Es un cigarrillo español, no?'

'Ah no, Marisa, es un cigarrillo francés. Gauloises. Have one.'

'Con mucho gusto. Un millón de gracias.'

'De nada.'

Initiating courtship via café Spanish and the chalk-blue crush pack of French cigarettes I always had at that time I didn't put much faith in, and so, on a wet and windy November night, I drove her to the room she'd got on the borders of Acton, hoping she'd invite me in. The house was a mid-terrace, in a tasteless painted brick, and with a peeling fascia betokening years of neglect. Its number I recall was an elegant 32, wrought in English iron and spotted with rust. She shared the house with two other roomers — a tall leggy blonde her own age, who went to secretarial college, and a slightly older single man who serviced computers. I assumed his was the bulky motorbike under a rain-sheet parked under Marisa's window, but I was wrong about that. This was not a point I appreciated until the fogs of winter had gone, and a cold April downpour ushered in the spring — all too belatedly in my view — when she did invite me in. However, that was only to look at some documents she didn't know quite what to do with.

3

UNLIKE ME – A young moneyed adult glad to be off-campus – Marisa wore the garb of student pauperdom with mystical relish, a metaphysics I never understood. This was a year out, she said, deciding then undeciding her degree course, an elastic that stretched to two years, then three, until finally the education option was a hard one to plump for, representing as it did an obstacle to all her other plans. Her subjects were French, English and history, whose hidden clues even I could detect, in the books that littered her room. That room incidentally was dominated by her bed, a king-size, with the floor space flanking three of its sides barely broad enough to tread with ease. We sat in the tiny kitchen, she with a mug of coffee she was careful spooning honey into, me with my caffeine plain (this I finally tipped down her sink on the instant she left the room). Signs of her two companions were the low insistent hum of a hi-fi directly overhead, and a torrent of bathwater filling the tub.

The documents she wanted me to look at concerned probate procedures and a property about to be hers, her grandmother having died and left it in her will. I looked them over and told her all she need do was wait. I looked up as I folded them away, and saw in her innocent eyes a cold blue intensity I hadn't much noticed before. Then indiscreetly I asked all sorts of intrigued questions, prime among them, where exactly was this property? That she met bluntly, with silence. No matter — time was getting on, and I searched my pockets for car keys. She led me to the front door and there hung on the latch as I stepped across the mat. Here I cast eyes on that antlered machine under cover outside her room, and asked if she'd ever thought to have its owner move it, blighting as it did the view from her window — which was pleasant if not spectacular. There was a small muddy lawn, a privet hedge, a half-dozen decorative paving slabs.

'What do you mean?' she said. '*I* am the owner.'

'Oh.'

Over the weeks that followed I missed a succession of Isabel's classes, first with a virus — it spread its flames upwards through throat and sinuses — and later with work at the office, where Bruce Senior (formidably patient, and endlessly diplomatic) had adroitly laid the ground for my nameplate, against a newly varnished door. Letterheads and calling cards I had in abundance. A revenant by now, I returned to my Tuesday evening class, mildly surprised and courteously entertained at the burst of applause my entry was greeted with. Marisa, I saw immediately, had

11

dyed and straightened her hair – through varying blends of henna, as she later explained – and was now a sun-dappled auburn. She was slimmer too, not that the dieting of that era was strictly necessary – a chicken breast one day, a melon the next. Then she'd somehow overcome the limitations of her floor space, to open up her wardrobes. Those long, loose-fitting floral skirts, and the cable-knit cardigans I knew from the winter months, had been banished to the improbable depths of her bedroom, exchanged for blue denims and a skimpy tee-shirt, all perfected to her shape.

Unobtainable as Marisa might be, she was – and in a flutter of eyelashes – surprisingly pleased to see me. 'Bruce! But where have you been!'

'Work. Incredibly busy. Contamos el dinero. It's company year-end.'

All things arcane in the sphere of corporate finance to Marisa represented a monumental waste of human ingenuity. She merely eyed me, I sensed with a grain of pity for the misfits like me, always at odds with a wider world of fashion or pizzazz. I tried to get her to meet me one evening after work, but she too was busy, she said, packing up her belongings and preparing for her move.

'You've got probate then.'

A smile confirmed that she had. I offered to help transport such effects as she had the few miles from her rented place in Acton to the house (in Ealing Common, I learned) that her grandmother had left her, but that wasn't necessary. Ex-boyfriends, way back from sixth-form college, had more or less formed queues in and around the parking lots off Hanger Lane, with trucks and vans and campers – all suddenly regenerate as eager removals men. However, I did get a call at the office, mid-way through the afternoon of her caravan east to west, with a plea for help.

'I can't think of anyone else,' she said. She'd unveiled her bike, but couldn't get it started, and now that all her things were in Ealing she was stuck. I had meetings that kept me for an hour or so, but found a mechanic eventually. A vast wodge of notes I peeled from my billfold, before leading him over highroads and back streets to Marisa's tiny garden plot. There I watched him chirpily lather himself in grease, and to a tinkle of spanners and other tools coax a first oily bloom of smoke from her exhaust.

4

I'M NOT SURE if Marisa's later amplifications did adequately explain why she was always so gloomy, at least when she hung around with me. I must have missed her mood from the very first moment, and again didn't detect it when we reached her new house, which I admired so soon as I saw it (its faded orange brick, and the grandeur of its gables).

'Why "Aspires"?' I said, puzzled at the nameplate.

The answer wasn't that simple. Her grandmother, having been widowed young, reverted to her maiden name – she called herself Miss Paterson – and lived an independent life. She claimed a distant connection with the Beaverbrook name, Lord Beaverbrook himself a man sixteen years her senior. She survived him by almost a decade, into 1974, when *I* was twenty-two, and Marisa not yet twenty. Max Aitkin, otherwise known as Lord Beaverbrook, certainly did aspire. On the other hand Martin Rae Miss Paterson thought did not. This was her good-for-nothing son-in-law, as she saw him – or Marisa'a father – whose only belief was in the fullness of his wife's

14

prospective fortune. But Ma Paterson held onto that, a not merry widow rattling round in a vast, unheated house, which now that she had gone had skipped a generation.

I saw the handful of photographs recording Martin's abrupt metamorphosis, a youngish man shocked to the grey of his temples, in a change that seemed to have taken place over the ten-day course of his honeymoon. Here in an album started in a decades-old September, Marisa picked out her mother with ease, yet identified her father more for his suit than his raven hair. By June that same two-piece had shiny lapels and was baggy at the knees — two emblems perennial by now — with its wearer seedy, defeated, and prematurely middle-aged. A first marital crisis was successfully postponed, when vows were renewed in a hotel in Boston Spa — this only the third anniversary of Rae and his spouse's union. Martin had renounced, he said, the last of numerous indiscretions, and was ready to settle down to married life. The point was even agreed contractually. Marisa, an infant at this time, did not travel with them — though nor did she stay with her grandma.

Unhappily for Rae, it still meant a return to the grammar school he taught at, whose jaded traditions he'd been complicit in for far too long, and conceits he abhorred — a philosophical position that was, according to one of his outpourings, as much to do with social conscience as any personal discontent. His subject was

15

English, whose literature he'd loved as an undergraduate, but since had systematically learned to hate, a small insight his wife could not have possessed, perplexed as she was at the lowbrow detective yarns he packed with their bags for the journey home. After this came another liaison — less protracted but messier than the last — which despite his contract obligations, or perhaps because of them, was one he willed his wife to discover. This time it involved long-distance assignations with a gym mistress teaching in Dudley, whom chance had thrown in his arms at an annual union congress, where one or two nights of passion prompted her to write him sloppy postcards almost every day for a fortnight. The thing fizzled out, and anyway by now the family thought it must act. Grandma Paterson left her house in Ealing Common, having first converted it to flats, and retired to a modest abode in the heartlands of Surrey. She sensed his disaffection with himself, and took him aside, asking him to manage both the property and its tenants, with a hint of bigger projects and more largesse if he made a good go of things.

That seemed to keep his interest, though not surprisingly he was passed over — for a younger, and much more dynamic breed of teacher — when after a bout of 'natural wastage' the head-of-department job fell vacant. His failure in that particular contest was outlined in a one-sentence paragraph, and arrived on his mat in a buff envelope, which, almost spitefully, an LEA secretary had not found the time to seal. His career was now as suddenly shabby as some of those suits he wore. Slight consolation came in the consultancy role he was asked to take on when an amateur production – of what was then in vogue, a Harold Pinter play – was planned for his local theatre. Not all wisdom had deserted him, and he was careful to keep his opinions out of the green room – Pinter: all the devices of dramatic climax, without an interweaving narrative. He did though have a fling with a divorcée from the wardrobe team, whose eighteen-year-old son – a strapping rugby prop – most artfully placed a breezeblock through the windscreen of his car (which anyway was about to fail an MOT). He got it fixed but ignored a leaky overflow pipe at the rear of Aitkin Aspires, despite frequent calls from its ground-floor tenant.

Other plagues visited that grand and lost domain. An outside drain, whose service cover one of Ma Paterson's handymen had removed years before, and not replaced, now finally closed its throat absolutely utterly under a mulch of rotten leaves. It overflowed spectacularly, flooding the garden, or desert, or wilderness, in a serum of soap suds, a bad portent a radiant sunset only made worse, pointing up as it did the tide of tea leaves left behind. Ghostly mysterious presences began to inhabit an upper-storey ring main, and manifested themselves as pale spontaneous midday table lamps, and with a dishwasher that churned into life so soon as you emptied it and left it

17

be. All these domestic ills a morose Martin Rae managed to ignore, to the point that the upper-floor flat fell empty, while the ground floor filled with squatters (loud music, marijuana, joss sticks). Conclusion: there was no money in property, perversely – at least not for him – and for this and other reasons his next amour was decisive. He ran off for good, having secured a publishing deal. Success had come, you might say, yet the minuscule advance he got, and a disappointing royalty, saw him emerge eventually as author of that well known *The Man Singer and His Sewing Machines*. For the entire duration of that great enterprise he holed up in Tintern, helping with the bed-and-breakfast business his new lady-love had struggled on with alone for over a decade – while in fact it was the man's missive, and not his mistress – his 'important' literary labour – that his wife, and now his ex, was humiliated by. Among the articles Marisa's father left behind was the appalling Larkinsquery he'd written in aphoristic verse, as a chronicle of these and other events, which one day I read and did not comment on.

Bleak, desolate lives.

5

FOR ONE MOMENT I stood there with Marisa, not as bewildered as she, but like her having no opinion yet as to where we might begin. I remember her thumbs, hooked a little dejectedly into the belt loops of her denims, a pair fresh and threadbare from the wash, and more faded than was usual for her. She'd got on someone's masculine shirt, a dazzling white and voluminous, with its tails hanging out, which made me think then (as I still think now) how waifish she looked. Her wrists, and for all I knew ankles, and for certain the lobes of her ears — all in such human relief to the ruin around us — were scented maddingly, in a perfume I could not know and would not identify now.

I looked around for the various service points, and turned the electricity on, and back off immediately when a shower of blue sparks followed its firework fuse across the ceiling of the vestibule, a trail that left dusty and ashen the one, naked bulb suspended above us. Much the same happened with the water, when incredibly, years after Martin's departure, that overflow had never been fixed. I do not follow a strictly linear course of events — I am not a

19

police – yet I did not doubt the man's insouciance by the time I had come to read his own account of things, as I happened on this in the margins:

Xmas, ho, ho, ho!
An icicle out of your overflow.

A white chalky stain to the back wall had penetrated deep in the limpid brickwork, and under the torture of all those unremitting drips – except perhaps in the frozen ambience of winter – the lower kitchen ledge had long been splintered into rotten little strands.

Marisa heaped some of the rubbish together, and swept with her booted feet some charred bits of furniture, one of several signs of conflagrations past – those squatters perhaps, freezing in a 1970s' February. The garden was a bed of weeds, with a wisteria, its foliage ragged, and scraggy, and out of control. Convolvulus trumpeted up and bound the broken fence panels. A mature apple tree centred the whole tiny plot – I expected something larger, yes – and was circled at its base by an attractive timber bench, which perversely looked and felt in very good condition. Here I joined Marisa where she sat, as blank as the darkish windows she gazed up at, they with a fluff of cobwebs blooming from the corners, she in a complex haze of her own.

'Well – what now?' I asked. 'What plans?'

She asked for a cigarette, though once I had lit it merely

fixed on how it discoloured her finger ends. Her first option was, she told me, to take off before the summer — just her and her bike and her bedroll — and motor down through France into Spain.

'I'll fill your first tank,' I said.

'Ah yes, but this changes everything,' she added.

'Oh?'

Her scheme was to sell the house, and with the proceeds backpack round the world — for one, two, five, seven years.

'I wouldn't do that,' I said.

'Why?'

I'm afraid I lectured her. 'Boom-and-bust as the house market might be, in the end the trend is always on the credit side — you can't have failed to notice. A place like this, if only your daddy knew — there's an income in it somewhere.' She wouldn't get a better start in life than that.

A troubled silence matched the near-contempt that filled me with despair in the way she looked at me, without saying anything. Then she stood, and stubbed her cigarette, and walked away.

6

I EMPTIED MY coffers over the following few days, buying in the people and skills she required, and tried to take time off – which proved difficult. I called in towards the end of week one, obliged to skirt the pyramid of bright copper pipes her plumber had abandoned on the threshold, and mildly surprised at how quickly the huge yellow skip on her drive had filled with debris – rotten plaster mostly, interlaced with old and suspect wiring. Marisa was home, or at any rate in, cradling a mug of coffee and seated dejectedly at a table she'd somehow contrived.

'Very resourceful,' I said, her kitchen centrepiece a door off its hinges, resting over two empty tea chests. Some few signs of how she'd tried to amuse herself were an open paperback spine-up in a box of vegetables, three or four loose sheets in a translation she'd started – the author French, and not a name I knew – and the first unhappy strokes of a self-portrait she'd concocted in watercolours. I picked up this latter and held it to the light, to the window, where a grey city sky did nothing to lighten its mood.

'You ought to get away,' I said. 'Or take a break. Anything.'

A few mornings ago my mother had reflected unusually long for her, and had quizzed me not about Marisa, but the work going on at her house. Faintly suspicious, and not able quite to guess at the purpose of her questions, I said I'd invite the girl over, and she could interrogate her firsthand. 'What do you think?' I said to Marisa.

'That's very difficult.'

'Why?'

'No wardrobes.'

'That makes it difficult?'

'Can't unpack. Haven't got a thing to wear.'

'It's you she wants to meet. In fact Bruce as well, Senior.'

'Problem is, Junior, I wouldn't feel comfortable.'

'Don't call me Junior. I'll hire an outfit.'

'You've spent too much already.'

'That's quite true, but don't tell *them* that.'

She sorted out a frumpy two-piece from the luggage strewn in the upper flat, its shade a bottle green that didn't suit either her figure or her complexion. I called home, to reserve an extra place at dinner, then drove her the mile or so to the seat of our family millions. Senior wasn't back from the office, and that meant the only car on the drive was my mother's – her little blue run-around – which to Marisa was hugely droll. In fact I had the benefit of many amused comments, all directed at plain, familiar things. There were the two swing doors to the garage, a little too neat and uniform (and gosh! electrified!). Then the porch lights, a matching pair, accessories more befitting a brougham (she thought). Final disapprobation came with my separate apartment, an extension built onto our house several years ago, Marisa's confirmation that effectively I still lived at home, and a part of the place I would not show her round. I did not appreciate her slights on my domestic arrangements, though I couldn't quite dismiss them as ridiculous – for example her watch over me prevented the removal of my shoes and replacing them with slippers.

Our evening didn't go that well. For its first half-hour my mother wouldn't be prised from her glass house, a point she not too subtly underlined in her distractedness away from conversation, we two beholding for our pains the meticulousness with which she watered her jungle blooms. Eventually she did put down her watering can, its long curved stem allowing one tiny drip onto the flagstones, where in the humidity it did not immediately dry. She swept aside a strand of hair and shook hands: 'You must be Marisa.' For once I found the polish on her interactions irritating. Bruce Senior didn't exactly improve matters, arriving late after a bad day counting losses, and intent only on talking business (difficult business) across the dinner table. That very forgettable meal I find on the contrary helplessly recalled, under the powerful beams

24

these hopeless mid-life reflections come saturated in. Marisa merely picked at her food, conditioned to all the diktat she so selflessly assumed in whatever her latest regime consisted of, preserving her youth. She declined dessert altogether, and drank her coffee *simple*.

All three of us tried, by whatever stratagems were natural to our life together at that time, to gauge her commitments once her renovation had been dealt with, with no mention of the sums I'd parted with to get that process underway. She motioned travel, though was careful, I thought, showing *me* in particular that plans for a seven-year trot round the globe had been shelved. She talked of her family only briefly (of her father not at all, not surprisingly), and of an enterprise her mother was involved in (to do with copyright research for authors) – a direction she also might take. Her uncle was in the newspaper business, an all-channel man for the nation's TV debating schedules – his politics transparently centre right – who in the years approaching his retirement edited a tabloid I do not care to name. Its opinion column was astutely monosyllabic, certainly not conceived on her own back route to Damascus, and had no correspondence whatever with Marisa's left-wing views. I watched, in the leaden deliberation Bruce Senior poised himself with, separating his cup from its saucer, and deduced that fleetingly he did consider this a likely vista for conversation, though characteristically did not air his

25

views, she after all an eighteen- or nineteen-year-old female, who to him did not appear to have work or a university. He did however rise to the challenge when he heard of Grandma Paterson's putative links with Max Aitkin, a man who stood shoulder-to-shoulder with Churchill in carving up the post-war world.

He told the story I had heard a hundred times, and was new to Marisa – of the widow, still a young woman, who arrived in nineteenth-century Paris, breezing in by coach, a vehicle groaning at its axles under the weight of gold, brought with her as bullion padlocked in a chest. Wealth, the measure of practically everything quantifiable, enabled her to start a bank, which prospered and grew, and was destined for success among the best in France. When eventually the widow died – a merry one, you'd guess – the chest was opened, and all these years later yielded up its treasure – not in fact bullion, but bricks. By then of course her purpose had been served, for no one would now deny her bank's credibility, the deception she'd wrought but one more human example of what authority over others actually is.

'As your Baron Beaverbrook also well knew, the fact that there has been deception is, in the end, irrelevant. The result is all that matters.'

Marisa corrected him: 'Not *my* Baron Beaverbrook.'

'No, of course. But it tells us where we live. Success will always wipe the slate clean. Failure is quite intolerable.'

'And morality doesn't come into it...'

'Morality is *always* a sore point.'

Marisa came to the house on one other occasion only, spontaneously, as opposed to coerced by me – a situation she never allowed to repeat itself. The day was a dead, gloomy Sunday. Bruce Senior and I were immured in the office at home, working irascibly, it has to be said, on a takeover bid – one of those bleak opportunities no one ever wants, while lacking the courage quite to cast it off with the day's cold coffee. Even then I predicted its failure, and must have regretted time I hadn't spent strolling across the common. She arrived in a roar of engine noise, and churned up the gravel, parking her bike where our triad of cars gleamed on the drive. Sudden interventions simply didn't happen, let alone like this, so naturally it brought a puzzled frown to my father's brows. My mother floated noiselessly before an upper window, fixing a gaze that drilled my back as I stepped outside, where I offered a cheery hello. Marisa ungloved and swept off her helmet, shaking out the curls in her hair, all a blonder sheen than had been the case just a few days before. Mischievously she waved at that figure upstairs.

'What brings you out here?' I asked.

Money had come her way unexpectedly, so she'd had her engine tuned – or in fact the whole bike overhauled – and was out in a first flush of enthusiasm, enjoying the breeze on her face.

'The forbidden fruits of capitalism. I'm encouraged,' I said. I felt able to tell her at last that I was having a new car delivered, a cabriolet, in only a few days' time, and looked forward to taking her out for a spin over the following weekend.

'A new car?' She sounded surprised.

'Why yes. The Mercedes – it's too sedate for a man of youth and charm.'

It must have been that final proposition she thought about, because Marisa hesitated not at all in turning down the invitation, a long cool ride I'd envisaged over coast roads, ending in a hamper plump with caviar, and a champagne I'd already cooled – one of those many presumptions I learned to live with the more ineffective my overtures became. Her whole weekend would be taken up, she told me, with a march to No 10, where a signed petition – including over a hundred celebrity names – would be passed across the doorstep, marked for the Prime Minister's attention.

'Supposing he's in,' I said.

'That doesn't really matter. There'll be news coverage – and that's what counts.'

'When shall I see you?'

'Perhaps in a couple of weeks.'

7

I SAW THAT Marisa's march, from Marble Arch to Downing Street – when I opened my curtains, and recoiled instantly under a glowering sky – would have to survive a downpour, which was only a drizzle just at that moment. I hadn't paid too much attention to her itinerary, not that she'd described it that well. As of most things with her, it had a certain abstractedness, with verbal embellishments more befitting an arts manifesto, and wasn't sufficiently clear to apply in a navigational sense. All right, I knew she was due to meet her three closest allies, feisty career girls digging the dirt in the cosmetology of glossy women's journalism. I didn't need, or wish to be told that a Hyde Park bandstand, not exactly the scene of good English martyrdom, had once seen one in that trio wave bras, banners and theological theses, one cold day at a corps of invited press. I couldn't guess at any of their garb for the day they'd chosen now, though wagered on the definite use of umbrellas, the four meeting up on that same triumphal spot (should a fifth have been me, I ask, a mere non-radical?). I hadn't been told the route to Downing

Street, and did not intend skirting round the Serpentine, in a shower of weekend rain, to find out.

I selected woollen slacks, a soft shirt, and a warm cashmere sweater, and breakfasted in peace. Later I saw the news clips, a brief camera pan across the jostle in from Whitehall, past those iron gates, its long regimental line made up not entirely of the grey-coated females I'd expected. One or two bearded faces I also counted. The thing went off peaceably and without much spectacle, their pennants ragged in the rain, and the drums, kazoos and klaxons dulled by the same good dousing. Their leader, a broad-chested academic smiling brightly under her halo, bore up the sacred tome – that A4 wodge of names – and uttered her lines to the sombre policeman manning the steps of No 10. Somehow that good officer spirited the door open, and thereupon stood aside while a servant of the house, a man pale-cheeked and darkly besuited, straddled the threshold and took the document in his arms. Hoots, cheers and chants. Then the newscast fluted on another perch – some insane mission into the Arctic – and was where I flicked the TV off.

I saw Marisa only once over the course of the month that followed, yet called often at Aitkin Aspires, to find her almost always not at home. When finally I found her in, it was under those first few hints of autumn debris that enshroud forever that brief time we spent together – a gust of wind and the rattle of leaves in her porch. She showed me round the lower-floor flat, its spacious living now transformed by its newly spangled decor – a floor lacquer, silken throws over all her soft furnishings, bright clean hues in a sub-tropic intensity adorning all the walls, and most of these hung either with theatre billings or reproduction Vorticists. A Spanish guitar propped up a corner on its stand, while a low table nearby was a hoi polloi of house or garden magazines, quirkily interspersed with back issues of *National Geographic*. A book she was reading, *Sybil*, spread its open wings over the arm of a yellow settee.

'I can see you're going to be comfortable here.'

'Yes – but it's not for me.'

Her first tenant – a movie technician – was due to move in at the start of the coming calendar month, and that would provide income for a finish for the upper floor. She took me there too, where life was still chaotic – the air dusty with crumbling plaster, new wires that ended in loops though never a light fitting, packing cases everywhere, and a bedroll spread out on the mattress where she slept. Last night's dinner I divined from an empty can of tuna. I told her she should try to get away while the last of the work was carried out, and of course – because I longed to suggest the new car, and driving her personally – I couldn't volunteer myself to supervise her workforce. All time stood still in the awkward silences between us, and just in the way she stooped to pick up that

31

empty tin I saw how impossible the two of us together would be.

I broke the silence, which now threatened monumental disproportions. I hadn't seen her for a month, and if I was in for a repetition – well, the next gap might as well be two. 'I'm in New York at the end of September,' I said.

'Business?'

'As ever. Shall we meet before then?' I turned to the window and looked out to the rear, where the apple tree had been lopped, and a collection of faggots, all smeared with rain and dotted with fungus, awaited the first garden fire.

'Call me,' she said.

I did, repeatedly, after several days – but then came a postcard, and with it an explanation as to why she hadn't lifted the receiver. Its juxtaposition of scenes, all in a kind of quincunx, was: an aerial sweep over Staten Island, a brightly lit Times Square by night, a chaise and its trotting post horses bobbing down Fifth Avenue, a signpost showing Wall Street, and the Empire State Building. On the reverse side, unsigned, but unmistakably hers – Marisa's bold, artistic hand – was the message 'Beat you to it' – all of which I binned, retrieved, binned again, retrieved.

8

SOMETIMES I GLANCE up from my morning paper, rattling in to work by train, when out on the platform, at the station we didn't stop at, blurs of autumn colours – dyes in the type of clothes I fool myself Marisa used to wear – briefly smear the window space, and that sets me dreaming again. The strides and the clumsy hobnails of the last quarter century are lost to the rose tints a simple house name on a list has crudely introduced. I go to meetings and am not quite attentive at the critical moment:

'What say you, Bruce? You're looking very thoughtful there.'

'Me? Ho hum.'

The minutes don't record that the notes and pen strokes I leave in the margins of the agenda are synchronised to the attempts I make at recalling absolutely all – the precise structure of Marisa's smile – how she held her head when she brushed her hair – that droop of her eyes if on a Sunday morning I found her slightly hungover. I know I have photographs somewhere, mementoes clipped to that sudden postcard from New York – Marisa poolside under a French or Spanish sun, reading, and always a very big book; her red and yellow scarf, tossed on the same March wind as a shower of pink or china blossom; her whole leathered being bestride her motorbike, her helmet dangling from the handlebars. I have some handwritten notes she concocted while she stood – one winter mid-morning, over a stove with boiling milk – thrown down on the reverse side of a shopping list she sent me to the supermarket with. Surprisingly they outlined plans for a piano composition – a talent I didn't know she'd got until, on the morning of her twentieth birthday, a second-hand upright was delivered to her flat. I search and I search, and I can't remember the tune.

And nor could I forget how on one rainy afternoon she dashed from the cab she'd hired and called at the office, long before my expansion with all our international accounts, and the move to central London. Bruce Senior, on his way out – his six-monthly dental check, I think – met her where our receptionist had led her to a seat, at her elbow a potted palm, and just in reach of the trade magazines her dress and general bearing must have shown she had no interest in (in the days when apparel went with your occupation). Bruce Senior was hoping I would make up my mind and offer my marriage proposals to the daughter of a circuit judge we knew, a bit of family business that did not inhibit his polite and charming words for Marisa, whom he hadn't seen for months but nevertheless remembered. She told him I had designs on the very ante-room they momentarily shared and were shaking hands in, and wanted to complement its light woods and Scandinavian furniture with one or two pieces of artwork – and naturally I'd thought of buying some of hers. She'd brought three samples, protected from the weather in a Harrods bag.

Two were outdoor scenes, centred on the same, broad, sandy horizon, over whose thick charcoal line holding up the sky Marisa had thumbed or smudged the strong vibrant colours of summer, a rage of citrus vapours representing beach huts, people, parasols. The pair hung in our bedroom at home until five, seven, ten years ago, when my wife, Henrietta, who had called in the decorators, used that moment to becloud them in bubble wrap and leave them with the lumber in the attic. The third was a figure – a reclining nude – whose collision of sharp angles and broad sweeping curves, and a blank robotic face, hangs among other items I've acquired and adorn my office walls with. Her initials float in the bottom left-hand corner – MR – and the date is, amazingly, 1974. All morning I have tried to remember the paltry sum – a small fortune twenty-five years ago – I paid her for her work, yet behold in those neutral features, which I see as a kind of self-portrait, only a painful reflection of that betrayal I felt when she flew to New York without me – or without telling me. The phone rings, doubtless there are emails I

35

need to reply to, Gladys has taken a highlight pen to all the day's documents I need to skim — yet all this disappears in a mist, and I think only of what never could have been. Snap out of it, you say. Don't you think all of us as deeply felt our first love?

Ah yes, but just like yours, mine was special.

9

HER UNCLE NUNKET, all through his own married life, and even before, disguised as indifference the plagues of disaffection he'd rather visit on his brother-in-law, in whose plod of weary failure he'd quietly predicted disaster — oh now years ago — though he reserved all that vitriol for the worldly subject matter swept over so expertly in his daily editorials. The man nevertheless held his niece in high esteem, and sent her cheques, food hampers, books his own people hadn't had time to review, plus several old bits of equipment his own household had begun to outgrow. I personally recall Marisa's hi-fidelity music ware, that piano I mentioned, and things as diverse as his pine-fronted kitchen units — these she got when her aunt refurbished that particular domain. I know also Nunk regularly took her out for lunch. On these occasions (and there seemed to be many) her trips to his office — all a meaningful bustle of busy newspaper people — would somehow necessitate a long wait in some degraded outer chamber thumbing through a pile of the day's rival publications (I know because I picked her up once myself from there, when a long delay culminated in a last-minute meeting Nunk was called away to unexpectedly).

Fateful (as far as I'm concerned) was a day in August, a time you'd have thought having few demands for a newspaperman, though in fact there were many. Some very energetic claims did in fact belong to that superficial season, and kept him elbow-propped at his desk, gassing down the phone. Driven, as ever, by the merry insouciance permeating his own column, the paper's gossip monger – let's call him Tarquin (a suitably unsuitable name) – was far from busy himself, and agreed to be both apologist and message-bearer, and set off for the waiting Marisa, somewhere in the darkness below. Something in her smile – and here at last is one of those finer details I fully understand…well, it bewitched and entranced him, and brought for example, on the instant of telling her her luncheon engagement was off, the news that rather it was on – but with himself as honoured stand-in for Nunk.

I got a good deal of this in slow, irregular beats, but only when my conversation with Marisa stuttered to its lighter climaxes, which were always rare. Tarquin had a penchant for earlier eras in cosmopolitan life, and having hailed a cab he whisked her away to a quaint and tiny restaurant he knew, tucked away in that charming labyrinth of streets fanning westward from Cambridge Circus. He liked it because it was as populous at eleven a.m. — which is to say not very — as it was at three in the afternoon, and preserved its exclusiveness through a hefty premium on its very extensive cellar. A twilit, or even dark interior was dominated by a central chandelier, and the tables, which were small, round, and intimate, were adorned with heavy linen — the napkins moulded by a specialist in origami, some days into sea shells, on others into scallops. It all depended on the mood outside, where the determining factor was always our London sky.

Happy Tarquin dangled his thinnish features, all led by a prying nose, endlessly over his bowl of minestrone, dipping a deeply bulbous spoon more often than it reached his mouth. A Dover sole followed, whose innocence and oval platter suffered alike those many exploratory incisions his fish knife made, all while his fork remained suspended. By his own special axiom there was always a crucial point of conversation important to get across to his young and impressionable guest. For example: what he didn't know about the McCartney millions. Or what a man like Hockney really thought of Mr and Mrs Clark, and not forgetting Percy (allusions I insisted Marisa explain). Or could she guess at the latest infidelity perking up that well wadded life of everyone's wine-bibbing libertarian, the Home Secretary?

A goat cheese he preferred to the sweetness of dessert, and a good dose of port. Marisa, never one to compromise her diet, I imagine picked at her rocket and chopped tomatoes throughout, with just a tang of vinaigrette.

'But then what about you?' he said, and wanted to know all about her ambitions.

Marisa? Why, she was destined for adventure, with a bag permanently packed and always ready for travel.

'Ah – for how that broadens the mind…'

Just then it became a working lunch, when one of the metropolis's least discreet fashion photographers turned up at last, for a meeting both he and Tarquin had postponed several times already. I'd heard of him vaguely, a man whose tabloid renown had propelled him with his lens caps through the mystical interiors of royalty and rock stars, nondescript as the man himself seemed – his plain brown hair, jowls very thick for someone of his youth, and a beard that had never thickened past an adolescent wisp. 'Of course,' and here I quote Marisa: Dill as he called himself – 'didn't you know? he's London's most photographed photographer.'

Dill (as he called himself) thought Marisa just perfect for the commission his luncheon with Tarquin was one stop away from, and so wonderful was that kudos attaching to his name that the man exploded onto the studio – later that very afternoon – with not only his cases of equipment, and a flunkey in tow, but with the brand-new model of his choice. I've seen the photographs. The arty ones are all in black and white, and show us an effervescent young Marisa Rae in the sumptuous nightclub costumes worn only by the

40

very rich – persons at that stage of my life tantalisingly out of reach. (They're two a penny at my garden parties now.) For the others Dill personally wrote her a sizeable cheque (his account was with Coutts, which in her mind put him in the stratosphere) then watched as in only a matter of days they entered that busy bubbling whirlpool of young professional women's magazines, whose emphasis was fashion and lifestyle. Casually she left them about her flat, a dwelling now of course overdue for the first of its internal facelifts.

Do I remember them, these glossy brooding photographs? Well, yes, the best I do recall, even to their distribution there among the chicest names in the clothes *beau monde*, and with them a haze of affluent perfumes. In one she wears a famous leather boiler suit, in others a roll-neck, sometimes with, sometimes without a white fluffy hat. There are several where she models a one-shoulder dress.

From here her flight to New York owed itself to a series of escapades and a long string of chance introductions, plus of course various other overlaps I find it all too painful to scrutinise, even now. All this redounded to her own secret purpose, and at first culminated only in the kind of studio sessions Dill had made possible, and later in something I'm still at pains to talk about, and which wasn't fully revealed to me until months after the event. It's almost incidental to say it was also much more lucrative, and eclipsed the need for my own chequebook in the renovation of Aitkin Aspires, though her income wasn't permanent.

When my own trip to New York was imminent I tried to get in touch with her several times – all to no avail. Such a busy life she led. I packed my shirts and suits, and everything else I'd need, and gathered together all those documents essential to my business there, and tried one last time to phone, in the five or ten minutes before my father drove me to the airport. No answer. Wearily, I tossed my case in the boot of his car, and with the radio tuned to news sat as a silent passenger, as we stuttered through Chiswick then on and out to the airport. Then in a whirl I was heading for the departure lounge.

'Good luck, son.'

'Why thanks.'

All I remember after that was a firm, vigorous handshake, and nothing of the flight at all.

10

BUSINESS SUCCESS I have never found that difficult. The deal I set up with our new traders on Wall Street enabled us to move to more prestigious office space nearer central London, which – if it hardly caused a smile – I was pleased about. Apart from actual negotiations I slumped into the awful routines of tourism, which brought me to my hotel bar at five every evening, where I drank too many gins, and tottered to the elevator – then up to my room – long after *hors-d'oeuvres* had been served in the dining room. Here in the insulated hush, with only a swish of air conditioning, I threw myself into the hollow of my bed and leafed dejectedly through the hotel information pack. Propped in my pillows, I phoned Marisa several times, without ever finding her home, then early one evening (Eastern Time), after my second shave, she at last picked up one of her newly installed extensions. There was a party in the background – music in a whirl from that inherited hi-fi – and the audio pyrotechnics of voices hooting at the stars.

'You sound very distant,' she said.

'I am very distant. Sounds like you're having a get-

43

together.'

'It's wilder than that, Bruce. Why not come over?'

'I would. Problem is, at this moment I'm looking out from my hotel room at the evening silhouettes over Central Park.'

'Ah – that explains the weird delay.'

The first faint signs of the illness that laid me low for a fortnight showed themselves a few days before I was due to fly back home. They'd turned into a full-blown something – 'flu, or one of my famous viruses – on the morning I sat in the limousine, waiting to be driven out to JFK. I recall, through the haze of pharmaceutical potions I'd dosed these last of my New York days with, how in the blooms of a very sore nose I tested a long dreary succession of Kleenexes, discarding an empty box number one well before baggage check-in. *Gesundheit* is what the smiling baggage handler said.

I took my seat above the wing and anaesthetised myself for practically the whole duration of the flight, choosing an endless ingestion of Scotch with ice. Not unnaturally I'd turned a dispirited shade of cabbage when finally the plane touched down, after cumulative loops through the ether (the runway when we skimmed to ground was wet with rain).

Then, infuriatingly, I emerged as the very last man on earth to find his luggage, the occasion crowned by the forensic deliberation with which I had scrutinised every

44

vagary and nuance of the carousel, going on and on on its ceaseless circuit.

Happily Bruce Senior never quite gave up on me. I found him skimming through a furrier's magazine, looking bored and forlorn, and not entirely comfortable on the bright plastic bench he'd found for himself. Not unwisely this he had chosen for its close proximity to one of those many TV screens, all pulsating every so often with new and newly confirmed departures and arrivals. I saw him glance up at it, a puzzled frown remoulding itself to a crooked smile once he'd caught sight of me. I explained what had held me up.

'Oh. Bad luck. You look terrible.'

'Feel terrible.'

'Come on. Let's get you home.'

I clambered into a very cold bed, and after five or ten minutes clambered out again, forced to answer persistent rings at the door, where under the storm porch, grinning very cautiously, my mother's daily help bore gifts and tidings in the form of a thermometer and a very hot water bottle. I took myself back upstairs, where under the whips of fire and icy perspiration an indissoluble grey kaleidoscope engaged its teeth and cogs through a multiplicity of changing images, all in a kind of Futurist delirium, which I tried hard to shake off. The shifting scenes it inflicted almost always had at their centre a persona I knew to be Marisa, yet whose looks were

45

antithetic to the wonder of her being, and cloaked in an enigmatic aura telling me to accept this vague new principle of life. She came to me open-armed in the stodge of middle-age, and suffering badly with gingivitis. Then as a disreputable teenager she planted one sugary kiss on my cheek, before collapsing into a fit of coquettish giggles. At worst she was badly overweight, with a weakness for gooey chocolate, one of those luxuries I knew she eschewed.

Our trysts and assignations occurred invariably under extreme conditions, and always in a bizarre locality. There was I remember a motor workshop, its whole capacity temporarily reprised to a gigantic, yet flaccid exhaust pipe, its needs critical, dire, remedial. Recurring too often for what sanity I then possessed was a Thames-side building site (some new skyscraper shooting up in seconds, in a whirr of worker-ant activity). Worse followed out at sea (worse always follows out at sea), where under a frozen spray of Shetland foam we tried desperately to talk above the din of an oilrig (what, pray, was our business there?).

She must have heard I was ill, because she phoned. 'How are you?' she said.

'Let's put it like this – if it now gets worse rather than better, the next stage is *rigor mortis*.'

'Would you like me to come over?'

'I'd love you to come over.'

'Shall I bring a priest?'

46

'Very funny.'

I relapsed immediately into that whirligig of deluded images, my diseased thoughts floating this time into the distant territories of extra-terrestrial life, where a race of people, much more ancient than our own, had burnt off their own precious eco-systems several million years ago. Some certain foresight had accompanied that destruction, and they had built not spaceships, but whole planets – with seas and hills and mountains and arable lands, and an atmosphere. These vast worldly structures came with built-in self-propulsion technologies, the plan being to voyage out in all known directions, so increasing what chances the race as a whole might have of surviving genetically. This madness I'd cooked up did have its certain underlying logic, when in a half-awake dream state I engaged with all the differing destinies these separated travellers – all of a common stock – were likely to evolve through, depending on what problems or opportunities they encountered. But the whole mental edifice tottered under so many offshoots and replications that eventually – my quilt cover damp with the fever I exuded – it all came tumbling down. What remained was a kind of global empathy I had for these very resourceful people – the cosmic gipsies *we* might have to become – cut off forever from their birthright, and condemned to wander eternally through the lethal emissions dusting the universe we share. Then suddenly I too was a cosmic gipsy, a man homeless, and never quite sure where to go – then of course the doorbell rang, and the nightmare tucked itself away, and there was my mother's help bearing a mug of stew.

I cannot be certain of what is now just as improbable a recollection – and one that still persists – of the moment I think Marisa called. I wring out the mental contortions of all those febrile days, but what I still don't remember – it's a blank absolutely – is all the practical mundaneness of hearing the bell, of putting on my robe, of letting her in. She poured me a glass of water, and emptied grapes she'd brought – the first of her gifts, for which she must have found my little Chinese bowl, which she rinsed in the sink. She told me her life had changed in oh so many ways. Then she put me to bed and prinked my pillows. Here I beheld her, perched at the edge of my mattress, smiling in that mystical way she sometimes had. Then she pulled down the quilt, and likewise the shorts I wore in bed, then having petted my manhood to the fullness of its pride she adjusted her own undergarments and raised the hem of her dress. This first of our liaisons must have demanded allowances as to the fragility of her patient, for I closed my eyes and mustered no personal effort at all – how could I, I was almost dead – yet learned to float and fall in that capacious heaven in every expert stroke, a testament of slow and perfected circles.

When I woke she wasn't there, and I doubted that she had been – yet *there* was the glass of water, there the grapes, and I didn't think the dampness of my bed was solely the fever.

11

CERTAIN OTHER INDULGENCES after this event — for me a hazy event — persuaded me it was not an hallucination, that Marisa, in the fullness of her femininity, *had* ministered the sick, and for one carnal moment had lifted me out of my frenzy. Naturally it wasn't something I ever dared refer to, or even hint at, in the course of our subsequent conversations, and neither did *she* ever allude to it. In fact Marisa was much more given to talk about adventures she had with other men she met.

I found myself looking back incredulously over this whole fantastic episode, and frankly not getting through the work I should, which Gladys only half jokingly attributes to middle-age crisis — a fiction, a cerebral rheum, I have never taken seriously. I find I can deceive her into assuming that perhaps I've snapped out of it, by asking her to reproduce that list of businesses, where the names Rae and Aitkin Aspires appear. There's a phony little ritual she always fluffs herself up through whenever we come to this, which starts with indignant pats to the petrified eddies in the latest of her hair-dos. She tells me how very busy she is — she really doesn't have the time to trawl through the vast electronic catalogue we add to every day in search of one particular name.

'Gladys. You haven't learned to use the software properly. I'll willingly give you five or ten minutes to show you how it's done.'

That represents a slight on her office skills, and three days later she produces a list — but not the right one. For me this has wider implications than all those purgatorial fires separating me, a man of almost fifty, from the salve I seek for my youthful aching heart. It's a matter of business efficiency.

I decided to take Gladys aside, and in a friendly sociable environment set out exactly what I expected of her, *while* she worked for me. I went in search of that expensive little restaurant where Marisa had prodded her lettuce leaves, regaled of her uncle's gossip columnist, a man who unwittingly paved the way for her media success. Over the intervening quarter century this as well as other compass points had gently dissolved under the atrophy of time, and I concluded it no longer existed. What I couldn't decide was whether it was now a pornographic bookshop, or the dry-cleaning establishment just a few doors from it.

In the end I settled for a more contemporary venue anyway, more to Gladys's taste, where without inhibition she munched her way through a burger and fries, brought to our table in the wake of her favourite test-tube relishes.

Mine was the poached salmon, rubbery and slightly overdone, during my tussle with which (a bent fork, a knife whose blade was several grades too thick), I explained that no business I knew ever ran itself. The purpose of compiling and looking at lists was to identify new opportunities — however small they might appear — and to seize them.

'Isn't that all down to the boys in the engine room?' she asked.

'Not all of them are boys,' I said.

'Sor-ree.'

'Never mind. In a sense you've got to the nub. That list I've asked you for — I'd like *it* and that new chap Lester Gravitt in my office on Monday — at nine.'

Gravitt in fact was not that new, having joined us as a graduate barely twelve months ago — though already he'd left a trail of corpses as the monument to his short career so far, which was up through the floors to my penthouse (spectacular all-round views I enjoy, which he would like to share).

Were I in any way persuaded by the Chinese horoscope, Gravitt I am sure was born in the year of the rat. He was a short man who hadn't yet cast off the shabby suits of student pauperdom, though the salaries I paid were competitive. His hair was a muddy brown, which arranged itself in greasy strands, plastered on his forehead. For a young man his paunch was pronounced, the natural handicap of thrusting males cursed of diminished stature. He always wore a buoyant smile, and had dishonest eyes. His gaze I never felt it fit to penetrate, and in all my conversations with him, which were thankfully few, I frequently looked away – a novelty for me (there is no one I can't face down: that is my first rule of business).

Gravitt's appreciation of long-term career progress I knew very well owed its essence to the curdled history of selected ancient Romans he patently admired, and the remorseless march of their empire. I foresaw I would have to let him go, long before his Brutus – on the same playbill and opposite my Caesar – managed to gnaw his way upstairs, where under the blind gaze of Bruce Senior's bronze he would one day smile that amoral smile, and somewhere in the shadows sharpen his assassin's knife.

He remained inherently suspicious, and because of that my plan almost failed – yet I did eventually deceive him, gradually, then completely, so that after several cups of coffee he really could say I had singled him out for 'special assignments.' Together we machined the list, which at last Gladys knew what to do with, down to its component parts, and with no subterfuge of mine saw Marisa's entry rise to the top. If Lester but knew it, his brief was the deployment of all those callous attributes I knew he'd got, and doing the thing that I had always hated – cold calls to potential clients – with Marisa high among his priorities.

'She looks the best bet,' I said.

'Why yes. With all those media contacts, there's bound to be a millionaire or two, just dying for our product range.'

'A lot of commission there, I think – if you can introduce yourself.'

Tantalisingly for me, his eyes suddenly brightened in a diffusion of all that inborn avarice that drives so many of us on. His chest also swelled, and having crouched with his ballpoint over the hardcopy we'd pared it all down to, he stood abruptly, reaching his full height.

'Okay. When do I begin?'

Not until, I suggested, he'd bought a couple of decent suits, some half a dozen shirts and ties, and shoes that didn't look so hobnail. 'Go and do that now,' I said. 'We'll put it on expenses.'

A few hours later he proudly reported back, sporting a line in heavy pinstripes I would not myself have chosen, though the shoes were genuinely elegant, the shirts modestly understated, and the ties striking without being garish.

'And you'll need a decent document case. Here – it's one I never use.'

Therewith off went Lester, out into the wilderness.

12

WE AGREED TO review Gravitt's progress once every fortnight or so. Alas the first of these get-togethers didn't go that well. The only firm who'd shown any interest in our product line was an uneventful management recruitment practice, its star client having badly mishandled important propaganda with one of the water companies, whose chairman's gilded throne had come his way after a recent cabinet reshuffle. Sadly some thoughtless news whippet – a maniac twirling daggers from the Left – had got hold of some volumetric reports, which showed a rise in leakages in direct proportion to the rocketing payola enjoyed by the shareholders.

Other firms in Gravitt's report were: a spurious housing association, a weapons manufacturer devoted to peaceful purposes, a 'really dynamic' publishing company, whose latest prize-winning hack had shut himself in a broom cupboard for ten days or so (a whole century might have been better), who between bouts of intensive masturbation committed to paper every delicious thought that sallied forth across the turbid crystal of his mind.

Result: more trash for like-minded persons to review on those proliferating late-night networks.

'Not very encouraging,' I said. 'What about that media firm we talked about – what was it called...?'

'Rae Agency – run by Marisa Rae.'

'That's right, Marisa Rae. Any luck there?'

'I couldn't see *her*, but did meet her daughter, Alicia.'

'Daughter!'

'Yes. It's a family business.' He glanced at Senior's bust. 'They do exist.'

'Of course. Go on.'

Alicia had met him under the misapprehension that Lester wished to enlist *himself* with the Rae agency. 'When I showed her the portfolio she said I'd have to talk to her mother.'

'And why wasn't that possible?'

'Well – she was home in bed with 'flu.'

''Flu! Now that is a coincidence.'

'How so? You feeling peaky?'

'No – I'm fine. Look, why not try this Marisa Mae again in a fortnight or so...'

'Rae. Marisa Rae.'

'Absolutely.'

I hoped Marisa's indisposition wouldn't keep her out of circulation for as long as mine had all those years ago, or keep her as confused once its cloud had lifted. I remember dialling her number just a few days after I had bid farewell to all those nourishing broths my mother had sent over in a tureen, Junior now a convalescent in robust good health, and ravenous for rare blue steaks. I let the phone ring a few times, but in a sudden inability to frame, even hypothetically, the question I most wanted answering – did you, did you not minister to the tortures of my delirium? – I crashed the receiver down, overwhelmed with fear and panic. Instead I turned to a notebook and began what should have been a playful billet-doux:

> Marisa,
> All in the myths of my conscience tells me your little bit of sylvan grove – Artemis and her haunted wood – isn't as Jupiter might have wished…

This first of my top sheets met the unrelenting vice of my white, and quaking fist, as it closed in around it, and a screwed-up floret ended in the bin. Another met the same fate:

> It's only acts of God and inexcusably careless investments that have shaken the foundations of my world, but now there's you…

That gave way to one last try, which I also trashed:

> So, the winning formula defies all those little conventions I've erroneously had in mind, the

> healthy handsome male laying bare the
> whiteness of his nymphet's flesh, serene on a
> sunny bed of moss...

I waited for chance interventions, and even then, when Marisa phoned me, all that crumbling mountain behind me – the past dissolving into Lake Oblivion, where an orange sun was setting on its waters – I left to its tender fate. Martin (that hapless father she didn't deserve) had descended deeper into Plato's cave, where the flickers on its walls were even dimmer than in Tintern. His bed-and-breakfast matron had fatigued like everyone else of the lassitude that bricked his path through life's practicalities – a fool's gold as paving material, his impossible destination an unseen horizon somewhere.

'Ah no. That,' said Marisa, 'is the artist's life.'

Art or not – and it seemed to me not – he'd been thrown out with his bedroll and bundle of papers, and had found himself a damp leaky cottage, wind- and rain-swept a drive away out on the Welsh Marches. Marisa had his interests too much at heart – an uneven reciprocation, I thought – and wanted me to take her there. So, by that alone, in the cold mizzle of a hallowed English Saturday, I'd at last got her seated in my cabriolet, its soft top firmly in place against the elements. She kicked off her shoes and planted both bare feet on the satin of my newly polished facia, and in a supreme act of boredom cascaded through all available channels on the radio (which I had previously set to news. Call me a stuffed shirt). We blipped through whole parliaments of outlandish sports commentaries, paused for thought at the plethora of popular music stations (professional interest, Marisa explained), and finally settled for an over-long hour on a women's discussion programme. Topics were: the removal of body hair; Freud's observations on proletarian acts of fellatio; the question, 'Why do men understand their carburettors and not their vacuum cleaners?'; Winston Churchill and the suffragettes; the essence of Iris Murdoch; plus a host of other things I do not care to recall (mainly barbed at men).

We arrived at teatime, though no such offering was made. Rae's unholy dwelling had a deeply flawed roof and damp stone walls – a sort of medieval cell. Some fool had built it in the depths of a very wet valley, where a yellow swirl of mist never got airborne, and the shrubs and trees and brackens were permanently filmed in dew. A river ran by. Rae, in deference to the rules of hospitality, tossed another damp log on his fire, which steamed and sneezed and finally irradiated jets of woodland smoke, the first of several domestic tragedies that drove me from his hearth. Marisa stroked his thinning crown and told him how courageous he was – then hideously the family smile I knew – until then only subliminally – pinned itself on his idiotic face. We were regaled, in the hardiest emotion Rae found it so difficult to muster, of the most recent professional *faux pas* he could bring himself to report on, a dirge he'd posted to Dr Larkin, whose office minion had returned it second class, no doubt curtly pointing out that the great man was too embroiled in his own flavours of urban melancholia to give much attention to the demotic affairs of others.

I set out in my car alone, having first retuned the radio. I couldn't remember quite how we'd got here, and missed the local landmarks, so, in slowing at every sign and turn-off, made regal progress over mile on mile of rain-blacked one-horse towns, the air heavy with the smell of wet flaming coals. At last I found roughly what I wanted, a one-man mini-market, where I bought tea bags, milk, bread, butter, some particularly greenish streaky bacon, and assuming we were staying for supper diced lamb in a cellophane wrap, some very earthy potatoes, and carrots plagued with anaemia – for a stew I would probably have to make myself. I took many wrong turns, and getting back found Rae in lighter mood, a man who could inform his daughter of the hits he'd scored, of the commissions that came his way (some novelty gift-shop publisher had reached the latter stages of negotiation for his *Zen and the Art of Sewing Machine Maintenance*). Wow! Well done!

I scraped away the charred remains of some centuries-old repast he'd concocted in his grill pan, and as the only one willing to eat – a too intimate ritual in the presence of a stranger – I made myself a bacon sandwich, having

60

breakfasted only, and ravenous by now. No such inhibitions constricted his appetites once we'd driven to the pub – a dismal, inauthentically beamed, and puritanical place, with very innocuous beer. A background of tuneless peasants, everlastingly camped on a jukebox I couldn't see, I deduced had somehow risen through the recording charts. For myself I ordered a single glass of port, accompanying that with a slim panatella, while endlessly plying an angelic Martin Rae with quarts of that local dishwater brew – his thirst made immortal through sachet on sachet of dry-roast peanuts. For Marisa I bought fags and a mineral water. After two excruciating hours of this, Rae had reached his Bacchic threshold, which sadly for him was giggling and adolescent. I drove them back, thinking about, but finally rejecting that stew.

Unapologetically – and with a smile I easily dismissed – Rae showed us the saturated chamber (with not a bed in sight) we were welcome to use for the night. Marisa, unflinchingly, was about to begin the search for sheets and pillows. I objected. I'd got papers to go through on Sunday, and wanted to drive back now.

'What's your line of work then?' Martin asked.

'Finance.'

'Oh. You're one of *them*.'

'It's getting very late,' his daughter didn't need to tell me.

'That's no problem really. Once we've hit the

61

motorway, west London's a hop — but you stay if you want.' That would have meant a train back for Marisa, and at that time of her life money she hadn't got.

Rae insisted on a send-off from his epic, an excrescence the wiser Philip Larkin had instructed his secretary to put back promptly in the mail — lines that Martin read, whose only recollection I have is this:

> The footsure Roman ran our town,
> Yet now our cocksure council runs it down

or

> If I were asked to invent a new séance,
> I'd hold up a test tube as its modern faience.

We left a little before midnight, the radio now retuned again, this time (once more at Marisa's behest) to a schmaltzy, nocturnal jazz, with a gravelly, sleepy voice introducing each new number. She raised, in equally distant, cool, caressing tones, the sordid subject of money, and how her need of it was pressing. I assumed this was all her mission of charity, and a familial impulse to relieve that frayed existence Martin Rae had heaped upon himself, a kind of Beethovenian hero (without the concomitant talent). Why couldn't he get a job, I thought.

'Ah no,' she said. 'Any hand-out from me...well, that'd be his final loss of dignity.'

I failed to see what dignity that was, but correctly didn't force it as an issue. I pressed on, prepared to drop her in Ealing, yet – miraculous to relate – she coaxed me to a coffee, which I drained to the sludge, and couldn't quite believe it when she asked me why not stay. Certain repetitions, stirring up that malady once consigned to the depths, recapitulated all those sombre leaden clouds I thought I'd fought off only weeks ago, when they'd first invaded my being. We showered. Then she led me to her room, whose uncovered rectangular window framed a velvet dotted with stars. She drew the curtains and turned on a table lamp, in whose warm and golden glow an enormous new bed had replaced what makeshift arrangement she'd put up with till now. I remembered her gift of grapes, and how she'd found my Chinese bowl, and the joke about the priest. Then, in that same reversal of roles, I found myself prone in the newness of her mattress, her tongue and lips and fingertips massaging every pulse, for thirty, forty, forty-five blissful minutes, my ivory-fleshed Marisa so expertly probing that threshold I had reached, with its promise or threat of one explosive emission. I moaned. I couldn't control my hands. Then finally she straddled my thighs, and with one exquisite downstroke fully absorbed that one last throb of fire.

A moody silence clung in her kitchen atmosphere when early the following morning we buttered our toast. I think I must have been confused, certainly regretful, and certainly slightly depressed – this latter sensation new to me – and all perhaps a physical decoction the essence of her own soiled being transfused into me. Why, I couldn't guess. I had to get on, I said, for I really did have papers I needed to go through, and I kissed her goodbye. Carelessly I'd left my driver's window open overnight, and under a light but persistent shower my seat was soaked. I thought better of stepping back inside for something to dry it with, and went through a whole box of tissues I kept in the glove box. Wearily I reversed out onto the deserted Sunday-morning streets, and on my way home marvelled – darkly perhaps – at the depopulated world that belonged to that hour, that day. One man walked his Labrador. A boy delivered papers. A few hopeless milk floats whined to a halt, restarted, whined to a halt.

I stopped at a newsagent's and bought a range of Sunday papers, after depositing in the bin outside my harvest of sodden tissues. Then I went home to a second breakfast – egg, bacon, tomatoes, chipolatas. That felt better.

13

NOT TOO MANY weeks after this Bruce Senior delivered the gloomy news that one of his regular check-ups had uncovered potential cancer of the bowel. A meeting with the specialist followed very promptly, who confirmed that's what it was – though detection was early enough that there was no sign of secondaries. Surgery went ahead, as did the chemo treatment a few weeks after that – which laid him low. Of course, I took over all aspects of the business – rather than manage just my own – and for a month or more this kept me at the office till ten or eleven at night, and often at weekends. I had not appreciated until this moment just how disciplined he was, and how rigorous, constantly sifting that vast hinterland that made up our accounts.

I became aware – sometimes vaguely, sometimes very fully – of the number of social calls all this bunker work kept me away from. Marjorie – one of Gladys's very distant predecessors – had firm instructions not to disturb me with calls not strictly business, unless from either my mother or father. I did on one or two occasions eavesdrop or overhear, when I knew that Marjorie was doing her best to explain this tough if temporary stance – to, of all people, Marisa. It was hardly a matter of indifference to me that in the past I had always had to phone *her*. Often I got home aching for my bed, to find among a huge catalogue of messages my mother had scratched on her pad several cryptic ones from Marisa – things like 'Please pick up your phone, before my coffee's cold,' or 'Before you know it, all my hair will turn to stone,' and this other one I remember: 'There's no eureka principle unless our bath is full.' These it seemed to me were more worthy inventions than the wretched couplets her father had inflicted on us both, and might almost have suggested she give him the benefit of one or two hours' tuition. Not without great personal restraint I did think better of it, and anyway it was always too late to call her back.

There was a lull, and then she changed her strategy, issuing formal invitations to premières of pieces she'd devised herself or was due to perform in, which initially I failed to take that seriously. Accordingly I offered humblest regrets. Things did begin to change after a month or so, when I was able to delegate much of my new workload to senior management, men and women I assembled one bright early morning in the boardroom, their younger representatives resentful, I think, unwilling to be summoned by a boy. That I didn't care to dwell on, though saw I must extinguish immediately a general assumption at the core of the group. With a fresh-faced and softer version of the boss – and all so laden with decisions – today was day one of extended vacations. They had this instinct for endless meetings, from whose minuted undergrowth the hardy action point systematically emerged as the perennial all of them depended on – that in turn giving rise to further rounds of meetings, and of course more points it was easy for none to action. I brought down my fist hard on the highly polished tabletop, and reminded them that this was London, not Volgograd.

No successful business ran as a democracy. I'd heard what they'd had to say. 'But this is what you're all going to do,' I said.

They shuffled their papers into respective portfolios – those who wore reading glasses slid them off uncertainly – and because by now I knew everything about the operation, the authority that gave me no one found easy to challenge. There were casualties of course. One, rather foolishly, deplored my power-crazed state, and cited only that as the reason for his resignation. Another disagreed profoundly with the departures I'd insisted on, away from the happy *laissez-faire* he wrongly asserted had characterised my father's regime. (Bruce Senior was a polite, and diplomatic, and inwardly a very hard man.) A third defected to one of our bigger and richer rivals. The whole exercise I viewed with the greatest satisfaction, having at a stroke rid myself of the worst of the malcontents, then establishing important allies by promoting rather than recruiting into the void they'd left.

I vividly recall a damp, blustery day on the cusp of that year's Christmas festivities, when one of my father's hospital visits coincided with an appointment my mother had with an eye specialist – so rather than she drive him, I drove them both. We dropped my mother first, then walked the huge distances, through a labyrinth of corridors, to the oncology department. There Bruce Senior slotted some odd few coins he'd got into a charity box, an object some aged Samaritan rattled under his nose so soon as we crossed the threshold. Talking of hand-outs, these he could see he must have had a weakness for, for having browsed through the company books a couple of nights ago, he knew – as I did – that we were in ruder health than ever.

'How did you do it?' he asked. 'And in so short a time.'

I thought about that. 'Um, well,' I said. 'I'm more overtly a tyrant than you.'

He chuckled. About the resignations, he uttered not a word.

14

I BEGAN TO have more time for Marisa and her exploits, invitations to which were now routinely wooing my doormat as part of her publicity mailing. The first of these that I studied seriously – once over my morning toast, and again at greater leisure on the train to work – was a flyer she'd designed herself, advertising Two Hats and a Hatter on Saturday night, at The Old Noah's Ark. The venue was a pub (it didn't take long to deduce), though no clues in her artwork – a nightmare Cubism in black and white and shades of grey – could help me guess at what her two hats and a hatter might be. On Saturday nights I usually dined out, often in a group large enough to dominate the restaurant, which as an indelible fixture on the calendar I'd begun to weary of. It wasn't hard to forsake it for once. The conversation was typically business, and much of the social interaction merely a preliminary to drawing up possible candidates for my prospective wife.

She, whoever that might be, would have to wait. I drove to the Noah's Ark and parked a few streets away in a residential cul-de-sac. The place was heaving, mostly with teenagers, though there were one or two of approximately my age or above. Over the one pint of beer I bought I scanned an interior of gentrified decline – scrapes and scars in the highly woven wallpaper – and a whole society's lung disorders symbolically marked on the nicotine-coloured ceilings. A half-mown velveteen upholstered three-quarters of the seating. The volumes were enormous – strata on strata banked atop our heads – yet the ventilation was poor, leaving swirls of languid blue tobacco smoke poised over every conversation. The wall lights were ancient timber fitments, with a castellated look. Many of the tassels formerly hanging from the little red shades left gaps, having gone missing. I shrugged. I couldn't begin to guess what Marisa was doing here, supposing I'd come to the right place.

Over in a corner, a balustraded, spotlit elevation, wreathed in a plastic vine, and so far untrodden by humans – at least while I'd been here – seemed the likely focus of what was to develop, though I couldn't help staring at the hook in the ceiling, way up above, where in a more gracious day a chandelier had hung. Cheers displaced the talk so soon as I'd made this observation, with tonight's jongleurs emerging from a dressing-room – a dark bearded man, thirtyish I'd guess, holding aloft by its neck an acoustic guitar, followed by Marisa, her own instrument an electric violin, which I greeted in some amazement. Both were in black jeans and tee shirts, the two hats (Two

Hats and a Hatter) a stove-pipe for him, and for Marisa a trilby, with a tiny crimson feather pinned to its rim, its rim turned down jauntily over one eyebrow.

Marisa could play, and well, as she showed by their repertoire, a medley of Irish jigs and reels, and songs I didn't know, or had never heard, for whose Dublin tenor (he mad as a hatter apparently) she would add a vocal accompaniment. The tics of her trade featured the flattened cylinder of a hand-rolled cigarette, which between numbers she perpetually had to relight, and among the wires and boxes connected to her violin a hearty pint of stout, which one of the bar staff regularly replenished.

Cautiously I backed away from the spontaneous bouts of dancing, when they broke out, though couldn't prop myself at the bar, which was always three or four deep with loud and thirsty people. I clapped hands once or twice, when I'd disposed of that pint, then feeling suddenly, and pointedly out of place, I left, well before closing time. I switched the car radio on then off (late-night critics re-inflating a whole sorry spangle of Westernised life in the latest musical to zoom across the Atlantic). In a couple of hours or so the streets would be a throb of all the merry hordes loudly deciding where to go next, though for now it was quiet and I drove directly home. Some days later, when I spoke to Marisa on the phone, I congratulated her on a surprise and accomplished performance, though she effected not to have seen me down on the floor.

'That's very possible,' I said. 'I didn't stay long.'

By now various tenants had passed through her lower-floor flat, which for the last few months had been occupied by a mature student (mature was twenty-six), a rosy-cheeked blonde whose nose was slightly *retroussé*, with a propensity for dungarees. (In the patchwork of all her stitched pockets I recall a collection of thick square pencils, which made me think of carpentry.) Her name, Xanthia, her mother had derived from a sun-drenched Eden somewhere – a holiday lost to the azures of the past quarter century, or now, as I write it, over fifty years. That's the hard thing about it all, all this vortex of time.

With a gusto her friends admired, and a boyish way of doing things, Xanthia was institutionally committed to the final weeks of her degree – she'd studied film, and the module now was scriptwriting, plus assorted adjuncts. She personally was breezy and optimistic, an inner stripe that must have helped in the remorseless strides she'd made – first-class honours everyone knew she was destined for. Professionally she wore a different hue, as a willing partner in the despair of her era, turning out great confections in her notebooks on the scourge of, for example, international terrorism, or the many practical problems faced by lone parents, or the defiles of a Western urban life no longer at ease with itself, then of course issues of governance and all its distant bureaucracies, and not forgetting that dependable, Britain's imperial past.

For her final evaluation piece Xanthia had co-opted a multitude of like-minded people, prime among them being Marisa, whose domination of certain camera angles presented yet further tracts into that part of her I didn't know. I was invited to Xanthia's showing (or a preview *before* the showing), a twenty-minute film she'd made, flanked on either side by a virulent home-concocted punch in her living room, and a less formal stand-up affair memorable for an endless ladling of chilli con carne — attended on a biblical scale by the many loaves she'd turned into rings of garlic bread.

I nursed but didn't dare sip that deadly student elixir, in the goblet I was handed, and found myself, in the bibulous preamble before the film, thrown into conversation with the few people there who were dressed like me. I don't recall their names, nor after all this time their proper job titles. Surprisingly one elder I engaged, a man with minutely combed wisps of sooty grey hair, proved himself irresistible to all the student life around us — a procession of happy hopefuls who, having noted my connection with Marisa, said hi or clapped me on the back, and begged to be absorbed into our hugely important small talk. The old patriarch, evidently, whose papal hand their lips would like to brush, had neared the cloud caps swirling at the summit of the British Film Institute, and so had the power to stunt or advance careers.

I saw the script repeated, if denuded of social content, with someone less than half his age, a man whose part-formed moustache I had looked at distantly and thought was beads of sweat. His tie was loose round his collar, with the short half long. Somehow the plays he wrote were screened on commercial television.

'You'll have seen them,' he said.

'No time,' I protested.

'But of course,' chimed the trio swooping for scraps behind me. It did them no good. His little-boy scowl told them no tips today, and he said only, when one of them inquired, 'To get on, all you have to be is a genius.'

Whether Xanthia shared his illumination we'd soon discover, for right here now, without ample warning, her floor was cleared and the lights dimmed. Most of us squatted down, pressed into cushions where possible, then in a machined hum and human hush her movie began. The scene I thought I recognised, from a dockside stroll I'd had with a once prospective client, a shambling if bountiful entrepreneur, in whose natural horizon the renovation of vast dilapidations – of mostly a warehouse complex – was imminent. Xanthia's interest in that same industrial wasteland – commercial in less a business, more a personal sense – was ostensibly social, the cast she'd drawn up just a smoky dream of ghosts, and the script she'd given them a minimal distillation of what a lost lonely wraith is able to verbalise.

Marisa, one of many, maundered in and out through the twisted bits of metal, the lightness of her tread in the dust and the broken glass betraying an ethereal quality I wouldn't normally associate with her. Half-dead people intervened – navvies, or office folk, or stevedores – and had as mental habitus the same symbolic continuum lived in by these deader ghosts. This may have been Xanthia's triumph, but what it made of their interactions was something cold and half meaningful, and however remotely grounded in the social mores we take for granted every day, here they were ghastly and sterile.

I queued heroically for my supper, shuffling into Xanthia's kitchenette, just as that elder statesman, hotfoot from the BFI, beetled his brows and prodded a tiny spot of garlic butter tumbling through his beard. He found himself, awkwardly, the appointed arbiter in a press of half a dozen students arguing for and against the film we'd seen. Marisa – who naturally knew all the answers, and as a healthy spectator liked to watch others seek them out – was only part engaged with the several litres of supermarket wine she'd just uncorked. In her purview were scores of plastic picnic beakers, all laid out on a chequered tablecloth, waiting for her to pour. I noted with pleasure that her hair was back to its natural henna. Unflaggingly too, she wore that exquisite smile.

'You should ask an independent,' she said. 'Bruce, for example. Bruce found it riveting, didn't you, Bruce...'

'I *will* have that glass of wine.'

'Cop out!'

'Cheers!' I said, and drank – a repugnant mouthwash not of the muscat grape.

Our grandee of the film industry helped me to swallow. 'In a sense,' he said, 'it's not the end product that matters. What you *learn* through the *process* of *making* work is *really* what counts.'

'Absolutely,' I concurred. 'Scrummy garlic bread. Very moreish.'

Someone sought a casting vote of the TV hack, as it turned out unsuccessfully. Someone else had seen him water a potted coleus with the remains of his punch, and forsaking the chilli con carne stride with a certain fire in his eye for the exit.

I remained long after Xanthia had done her washing-up and had vacuum cleaned the vacated living space. I did not offer to help, and from my cosy vantage tried to puzzle out – because it struck me as incongruous – how like a farm girl she looked, or rather how in an air of combat she battled through her chores. Marisa – who unlike her tenant possessed a filter jug – made three mugs of coffee upstairs and brought them down, then finally had her deliciously wicked way when she led me to her lair.

15

MY MOTHER, THE most objective person I know, should never have to fret that a bright successful son was also lured by dark mythologies, whose suitcase had already been packed, his wallet oozing both banknotes and the ticket he'd bought to oblivion. She was however thorough – even forensic – in setting out her view that family negotiations, mostly in respect of Henrietta, did demand discretion. That was fine, I said – for I am not in principle opposed to arranged marriages. But – Marisa was more to me than a sentimental attachment, and there were genuine moments of love that we had.

My mother did in part understand this. 'You can always keep her on,' she said, meaning somewhere in a depth of shadow, while I made the transition. What she didn't appreciate was 'keeping Marisa on' was now a routine difficult to interfere with. Regularly happening between us was a kind of frenzied mechanical coitus, she perched on her kitchen table or chest of drawers, depending on where we were. Always after that event she showered immediately, and, I noticed, spent time and effort on a complete change of clothes. I wondered if these weren't habits I was likely to regard at the social remove my mother had in mind, or dispassionately.

We move on, or back, for in those complex days one of our newer business friends lived with his wife and teenage daughters in an attractive ivy-strewn property tucked away in Denham. I well remember the name of the firm (eternally a changing compound), and the none too subtle point that he was a senior partner. Consciously he'd made it synonymous with royalty, by telling me several times that it handled the Queen's accounts. For all I know, its present reincarnation still does – though I really couldn't say. He and his wife invited the three of us to one of their regular evenings, always noted for the quality and distinction of their after-dinner speakers. By an amazing coincidence, the one they'd hired for this occasion – which might have been a birthday – was that grand old man from the BFI, whose last appointment (at Xanthia's) he'd doubtless already put from his mind. Not less seedy in evening dress, the starchy depth of his shirtfront only accentuated the coffee-coloured stain of his trimmed goatee. His name was Richard Adlam, MBE.

My father was much too ill with his treatments to contemplate eating at all, let alone at someone else's table. My mother of course would not desert him. Therefore it was left to me to carry our banner into the bowers of Denham, where over the pre-prandials, in a drawing room

spectacularly lit by moonbeams, I made more than mere
diplomatic effort to engage Henrietta in conversation. She
was taller, larger framed and bigger boned than Marisa, yet
still elegant and slim. For her nights genteelly got up, her
reddish brown hair was gathered from the nape of her neck
in a complicated pattern of ringlets, and the dress she chose
was always *décolletage*. She'd loved the south from her
childhood, and still spent several months a year in one of
its sunny resorts: whatever the English weather, Henrietta
was always lightly tanned. She spoke expertly on French
cuisine, and wore denims and wellingtons when driving
her Landrover.

'Henrietta – so long since the last do.'

'I can scarcely remember, Bruce.'

'And isn't this surprising – Denham – tucked away
here.'

'You'd never guess it was, driving past.'

'Apparently one of those chaps from the English screen
lives hereabouts.'

'Yes – he's over there, talking to Freddie.'

'Ah, you knew!'

'But can't remember the name.'

I did not pair up with her again until after Richard
Adlam, and then had to wait some forty minutes after he'd
bashed his wine glass. He rose, in an exact synchronisation
with the arrival of the cheese board, and without a twitch
or clearing his throat embarked on a handful of carefully

scripted anecdotes. The gist of these I have to admit is lost
to the swamps that act as repository for the days before my
marriage. There was something about the Boulting
brothers, and an art collection. Then the little known fact
that Alec Guinness was really a very unhappy man, who
loved only his dogs, and whose mother would not reveal
his father's identity. I can remember coating a water
biscuit in wedges of Brie, while Adlam told us how he'd
mediated – 'oh, a good many years ago' – when Marilyn
Monroe, with her husband in close attendance, had arrived
in London to work with Laurence Olivier. 'Dear, dear
Larry.'

Then we all learned why Richard Adlam *was* our after-
dinner speaker, one of those gentle revelations I took with
a glass of port. At times he rambled chaotically, and then
I'd notice the sliver of Stilton crumbed and compressed on
the blade of my fruit knife. However, here it was – his *pièce
d'occasion* – the startling disclosure that here – right here in
this room – a scene from one of those gloomy Fifties'
thrillers had been shot, with Adlam himself on the
production team. Hard as it was at this remove temporally,
our culture shaken into all sorts of kaleidoscopic changes
since those days, what we should try to imagine was the
broad patio doors to his rear, now concealed against the
night, with its ten o'clock moon, just inches behind that
velvet depth of blue in the curtains. 'Ah yes, curtains.' The
film counterpart of these was a billow of windy lace, the

doors opening not, as we all knew was real, onto a suburban terrace, with its patio, lawns and parterres, but into the chilling unpredictability of a remote English moor. In film work locks and latches are never enough to withstand the growling elements. There's a gust of wind. There's the menace of a cello and piccolo, playing a duet. The doors fly open. All our stilted luxuries seem to dissolve at the moment the lace curtains fly. Then the music ends suddenly, breathless in its climax, and the soundtrack finds its other gear. There's a something, a deeply monstrous something, throbbing on the moor, whose opposition to us rises in a howl. With that our whole cosy notion of what civilisation is, is undermined.

By one of those random acts that stick with us forever, grossly over-emphasised – in my case the very erasable trauma of all my wisdom teeth removed – I was delivered, some years after these events, into a convalescence overseen by a loud, gigantic television set. This when I first encountered it was doling out its discourse to no one in particular. My arrival ended impatient liaisons with all its channels, followed by the kind of consensus no one ever voices. Hereafter I cradled my chin and settled down uncomplainingly with three or four other post-ops. Perhaps not amazingly after all, it took me a while, and some effort with the banality of its plot, to grasp that the film I was watching had given the MBE his after-dinner limelight. I could not help but see what verve there was in its fiction as something he merely talked to us about, which was a great relief anyway. Till that moment came, the jellied gore I'd had to put up with, in the conversation I'd overheard (an eye surgeon, a few table places from me), had turned my Denham dinner into a minor effort of will. Here for me alone, one of Ealing's great filmic moments – and don't forget, I'd great Ealing moments of my own – was the terror-stricken face of a hapless victim of *something*, crashing through those doors and sprawling on the hard stone floor (in truth a glossy orange parquet), just where the dining table now was. A part of me wished to blurt out that I'd seen it all before (so to speak), though the thought of all the numbed sentences *that* would entail pressed me back in my chair, massaging my jaw.

The party in Denham began to find its natural end shortly after midnight. An older man I hadn't met before had watched me fumble through my pockets, and to save me the trouble – all clearly etched in my expression – swooped with his cigarette lighter, and there held its flame to the cigar I had just divested of its cellophane. He introduced me to Richard Adlam, now circulating merrily, slightly pink at the jowls, and swishing a brandy clockwise in its glass. Handshakes, and a puzzled, inquiring look from him.

'I know you from somewhere?'

'I don't think so. Those were wonderful tales from the film world.'

'Glad you enjoyed.'

'The public image unveiled. I'm especially surprised at Olivier.'

'Well — there are things I *couldn't* tell.'

'I bet.'

I spoke briefly to Henrietta's father, who always wanted news from the stock exchange, and to Henrietta herself as I escorted her out to their waiting car. Mostly I recall the mingled scent of the perfume she wore, the cigar I smoked, and a cedar tree silhouetted against the night, when I confessed that the time had long passed to invest in a hearth of my own. I'm too well aware, as I reflect on it now, of just how carefully I chose my words, describing this planned foray into the maze of real estate as the search for a bachelor pad — though she knew very well I meant marriage home.

'Exciting,' she said. 'I do so love house hunting. Want me to give you a hand?'

I held the door as she settled into her seat, thanking her very much for that and promising to ring, then closed it with a gentle clunk. A mild gust of exhaust followed the throb of the engine, as smoothly, and without much noise, their big black Bentley began its return journey into the Oxfordshire countryside.

What had I done?

16

IN FACT I allowed several days to pass before I made that call. I used the time to gather a small portfolio of property details, then watched with alarm as my diary filled with appointments. Thereafter I'd meet Henrietta for afternoon tea – these were Darjeeling days, she with her coconut macaroons – as we planned our routes through the various addresses agents or owners were keen to show us round. That whole viewing episode passed in the same depressed state as the properties themselves – homesteads in the limbo of their occupiers, gone or moving out. Nor could I ever learn how to chat affably in a bedroom potentially my own, while gazing down on a garden darkened by aged fruit trees, or try not to look dejected at the cluttered Victoriana late of some nonagenarian, a crock or crone heading for a care home. Sometimes I looked incredulous at the kind of extensions my fellow-Englishmen were apt to build – Edwardian elegance marred by a 1960s' flat-roof utility (to quote only one example). To console myself I did consider one possibility – which incidentally Henrietta adored – not too long a walk from Ealing Common, though rightly foresaw temptations, and a blight on the marriage I knew I was about to embark on. Miraculously I drew up a shortlist, which according to Henrietta was topped by a vine-entwisted, seven-bedroom family home just a short walk from Chiswick House. She liked the bustling High Road, and (I suspect) the ease of access to the West End, to the airport, and to the motorway back into rural Oxfordshire. My own personal favourite was a stunning riverside property in Hampton.

I sifted through various mortgage deals, and I paid attention to all those arty invitations bearing Marisa's name, when they chanced through my door. One in particular intrigued me all day long, and by dinnertime I'd decided to go. This was after her Irish partnership had been dissolved – I can say I *am* very confident about that epoch. That is because – whether the money wasn't good, or there'd been a falling out – she'd left the pub scene, and in its place had formed a trio. Its other two members had names I didn't recognise, and anyway I can't remember them now. But one thing was clear: money had come from somewhere to finish off her flats, but that was all gone and now she needed more.

It infuriated me that she'd never scrutinise a balance sheet, and I am tempted to say that her practical deficiencies of that time were the conscious foils (for me) prevailing in all of her doings just at that moment. A good case in point was the blurred photocopy whose origin was an old, dog-eared *A to Z*, tacked in as an inset to this latest of her mail-outs, supposedly to show us how to reach the obscure performing venue she'd hired for her evening, somewhere in the back streets of Hammersmith. I must have spent half an hour circling the relevant signpost, shunting up and down the wrong blind alleys, then almost giving up when forced to reverse from a one-way street. In the end it was one of those easy flukes that ensured I found my seat, here in the gloomy cavern her trio had chosen for its debut, a puzzle I failed to resolve in the few dead moments before the lights are dimmed and people cease to shuffle in.

There were several reasons why the event itself was memorable, but as a concert was instantly forgettable (I speak for myself). As with her Irishman, Marisa had chosen black, which under this new musical horizon had transformed itself to an evening dress – moreover one that hugged her thighs and was hemmed acres above the knee. It coruscated dazzlingly under the lights. If at the same time you asked me what the others wore, I couldn't say – for still I had eyes only for her, despite Henrietta. I recall very clearly the instrumentation (which as I understood it varied from night to night). There was Marisa's electric violin. There was a prepared piano. There was percussion. The latter was used sparingly – a gong, a glockenspiel, chime bars and cow bells. I read all this several times in the programme notes, no doubt asking myself what next. Soon

I found out, when all the pieces they played were an unremitting cacophony, which as I explained to Marisa afterwards was too advanced stylistically for a man of traditional tastes. Ironically she accused *me* of artistic affectation – not that I didn't understand these new orthodoxies Marisa was always interested in.

Certain external effects were introduced twenty minutes or so into their performance, I suspect as a relief to the tedium others like me had begun to experience. Large bundles of balloons were released from the gantry, at no great height above the tiny performance space, some pink, and some a pale maroon. It was hard not to think that individually their random fates were a concretisation of the notes being played. Any I saw bobbing innocently on the boards were likely to meet an explosive end under Marisa's booted feet, an action sprinkled with usual erotic overtones. Others that escaped, and floated over our heads, were stoically ignored by men like me, while people around me made a grab, or bunched their fists to deliver a blow. I tried to be polite about it, in the loud dingy bar we met up in afterwards, though without concealing the truth of my opinions. Her arguments, usually playful (if in a slightly condescending way), tonight were injected with a passion I hadn't seen before.

'You can't just say it doesn't work,' she said.

'I'm not exactly. It's just that to my ear it's all a bit too – well, labyrinthine.'

'Labyrinthine?'

'Yes – talking of which, just last week I tried my luck in that maze they've got at Hampton Court Palace. You ever been there?'

'Don't change the subject. What were you doing in Hampton?'

'House hunting.'

'House hunting?'

'Well why not?'

'At last you take my advice.'

She couldn't say these things without her little sneers, and without these cutting remarks, though the smile on her face betrayed not the slightest hint of malice.

'It was planted in the reign of William III.'

'What was?'

'The maze at Hampton. They say probably with hornbeam. It's holly and yew today.'

'That's fascinating, Bruce.'

'*And* I know the key. What you do is go left when you enter, then take the next two right, but always left after that.'

'I'll bear it in mind. What sort of house is it you're after?'

'Any I can populate with hundreds of children. Interested?'

'Not in children.'

'That sounds less a no, more a caveat.'

Marisa only smiled. Perhaps that was right, when only a few days later the house in Chiswick fell under the auctioneer's hammer, and with my signature fresh on the dotted line a mortgage was approved. To my mother it was all straightforward, yet for myself I could not anticipate clearly which of the two it would be, destined to drag me through all the usual department stores, my credit card flexed for the vanloads of furniture about to be delivered, and with an eye to all those other accessories that suddenly assume importance. But of course it was bound to be Henrietta.

17

A RING OF mystical bells, very pronounced in a spate of difficult dreams that began to interrupt my nights, Marisa felt certain had meaning, and without any prompting produced several unlikely theses in support of that view. When I asked her what made *this* one of her subjects, she named a tabloid astrologer. This was someone she at first said she knew, then knew of, then merely had information on. All this seemed no more than the Fleet Street gossip that, through her uncle, she was privy to, even if certain things turned out to be true. For example, it did seem to be the case that on a daily basis her Mr Mantic telexed all twelve texts, all twelve of his diurnal flights with the zodiac, from the Greek island where he lived to the newspapers that syndicated him. There was a long string of books to his name, all of which had been on the bestseller lists, and two of which Marisa had on her shelves. They were wedged, I couldn't help but notice, between a Tolstoy and a Somerset Maugham, no doubt late of her father's library — not that I took that as a decent explanation. Book one had bells in dreams as indicative of homecomings (one thought of cattle meandering farmward down an Alpine slope), while the second – a later publication – thought they were more to do with all last things and summings up.

In hindsight I might have mused how lucky a forecast option two appeared to be, when on a weekday, at 5.30 a.m., as dawn approached, the sky a cold-looking hammer-beaten band of lead, my bedside telephone tinkled away insistently – first in the ghoulish environs of the office nightmare I was going through, then as was actual, at my pyjamaed elbow. It was my mother calling from next door, and I went round immediately.

Here I saw grimly what had happened, whether true to my pealing bells and Marisa's stars or not. Bruce Senior hadn't been able to sleep, and at four o'clock finally, having pulled the covers into a thousand misshapes, had slipped on his dressing gown and gone downstairs to make himself a cup of tea. A few things from the night before still littered the space in the living room, where he came to sit down – a broadsheet folded at the city page, the TV listings, and on the arm of his chair the A4 pad he'd been jotting down some business on. We – my mother and I, and the doctor, here before I was – saw all too clearly how he must have planned for a lengthy stay, despite the cold, having dragged from a hall cupboard a dozen or so large boxes full of family photographs – practically all that were ever taken during my life, and some pre-dating that.

Remarkably he'd sorted through hundreds already, in a meticulous process lit only by the soft tasselled beams of his standard lamp. Even more surprising, those he retained – and here they were spilling from his lap, over his slippers and onto the floor – were all of me, in every stage of life, man, boy or infant. If I wasn't alone, I *was* the central subject.

There remain many reasons why to Bruce Junior these are still semi-sacred objects, which I keep even now, just as he selected them, in a large leather file of my own. I try to keep at bay those disabling moments of family nostalgia, even when life with its long office hours is drear. If, sometimes, I gaze into the eyes of my own progeny's photograph, perched on my desk at work, then up at Bruce's bronze, it's always with curious disbelief. I know I'll be maudlin for the rest of the day, and my leather file with its snapshots will be visited that night. I know too that the history of how Marisa was always impossible for me is written there. Look, I will say. Here I am as a moping, slightly bewildered four-year-old, astride a glittering new tricycle, pausing for the lens on a deserted, poplar-lined track somewhere in northern France. My hair is now thinning and a nondescript dun colour, but then it was blond and tousled. From any others I randomly select it's clear I never really smiled that much (I can remember feeling oppressed, if I couldn't put that word to it). As a seven-year-old I spent a week in skis at an expensive resort in Switzerland, but the look is unpleasantly studied. At nine, in Mexico, I was urged up a rock face, with all the tackle and instruction you'd need, but here I'm as bleak as the climb itself. A faint twitch does invade my lips when I scooped a first prize at school for maths and physics, when as an earnest fourteen-year-old a primer on Planck had convinced me that the universe was not as Einstein had suggested. That brief fire in my evolving mentality dulled and cooled into the study of stocks and shares and the business world, and a look into the workings of government and parliament. Bruce Senior was pleased about that, though disguised his disappointment when degrees were handed out.

I am never persuaded that life for a man is the unspoken denial of the person his father wanted him to be, or tried to mould him into. I feel I did have some choice in the matter, though in exercising that choice introduced differences between us that neither of us ever repaired. My one regret now is that I found him dead in his dressing gown, reflecting on his heir, in a departure leaving everything about that heir still unresolved. Nor was I very much pleased when the doctor took me aside and described the nature of his death. It wasn't, as I'd often thought it would be, cancer that had got him, but a heart attack, 'massive and enormously painful,' according to the GP – not our regular one, but someone new to the practice who that night happened to be on call.

'Thanks,' I said, 'but I wish you hadn't told me that.'

'I'm so sorry.'

'Don't whatever you do repeat it to my mother.'

Yet my mother was strong. In the days that followed I made a start on his paperwork, while she arranged the funeral. What I didn't know (until the bronze was cast) was that while I totted up his shares, and combed his accounts, and sorted out his various insurances, she'd organised a death mask. That was even when, from time to time, I did get up from my work, usually to tell her I'd thought about it again, and would delay my move to Chiswick.

'No,' she said. 'You mustn't do that. It's even possible I will move.'

This mantra she repeated whenever I raised the subject. She's eighty-one now, very nearly eighty-two, and she remains there still.

18

AFTER SOME CLEVER little subterfuge on my part – or so I thought – I spent a solid hour one sunny spring afternoon showing Marisa my new Englishman's castle, not nearly so majestic in its sudden state of undress, its vendors having removed their every last possession. We followed the contours of the house, as did the conversation – bright and effervescent in all the rooms that had large, south-facing windows, where the sunshine lit the dust our footsteps raised – but slightly troubled in the blank square thickness of the hallway, where Marisa told me frankly again she needed money.

I asked if her problem was debt, but that was definitely not at the root of it. Who hadn't got debt, she said: hers was manageable. Her pressing need was the outlay for one of her projects – a feminist tract she'd produced and wanted to publish all over London. She explained, because this was not an industry I had dealt with or ever thought about, that in an age of celebrity the dissemination of intellectual artefacts ran to much more than simply the production costs. The transaction she had in mind was not just a case of setting out her shop front. It involved PR people, without whom radio interviews, and a splash in the world of high-gloss magazines, weren't that easy to acquire.

'So what you're saying is, a career in media is something you have to buy into...'

'We don't all have daddies who laid down a career path for us.'

'That's shockingly insensitive, given I've just cremated mine.'

'It wasn't meant to be personal.'

We moved from the hall, with its angular depth of shadow, and stood for a moment at the vacant centre of what in future years would be my family breakfast room, a shell that for now had satin yellow walls checked with the shadowy rectangles left behind by the pictures that had hung there. She stood with her arms akimbo looking out through the polished glass of the patio doors, beyond which a matrix of terracotta tubs – in a kind of purposive randomness – disrupted the regular pattern of flagstones. After that was a large walled garden with grass that needed cutting.

'Bit wild out there,' she said.

'I'll get a man in to sort it out. Don't suppose you see any of this as a happy harvest domain, with lots of bonny children at your feet...'

'Bruce, we've been through that before.'

'I shall find life very hard without you.'

'We'll be friends. I can be godmother to your firstborn.'

'I'll hold you to that.'

Her next prospect of income, beyond that staple, the rental of property, was the exhibition and sale of selections from her artwork, from a gallery she'd hired for two or three days in Bayswater. This mostly was figurative – some of the nudes I'd seen, with elongated limbs and very large hands (after El Greco, she said) – and all of them aspects of herself. Others I hadn't seen were designed to overreach their frames, and these – not I think autobiographical – were strangely truncated at various points above the knees and elbows, and were sometimes headless. Her materials for most of these samples included charcoal, water-soluble pastel, acrylics, with a technique that usually involved a layer of wash (or at least that's how I think she explained it).

When not working with figures she liked to play with primitive perspectives, a notable effect in the charcoal-on-paper she'd labelled *Garden Furniture*, a surreal collection of objects resembling those she must have remembered on looking out from my parents' dining room. Another, *Interior with Gin*, was her own kitchen, but seen through a rusty veil, and stripped of all bar a stool, a small round table, and planted on it off-centre a bottle of Gordon's.

I managed to take in Bayswater towards the close of the

second day, the venue a white interior with tiny spotlights dotting the ceiling. Background monotones were a recorded piece by a man called Stockhausen (I was told). Little red spots gummed to the index cards that named each hanging denoted which had been sold. There were still quite a few that hadn't. I browsed around the place, not having caught Marisa's eye, the catalogue someone had thrust at me rolled to a tube, and clutched in both my hands behind my back. A tubby little man in a business suit, and with savage green eyes, and his voice a surprised falsetto, all too abruptly opened negotiations for a discount, having shown interest in two self-portraits. To *my* amused ears, and perhaps to mine alone, it was all too tortuous a rigmarole, he not really wishing to buy – he was asking for twenty per cent – and Marisa more a special case than he might think.

'We aren't a charity.'

I sought refuge in the catalogue, whose introductory page was written by a young Michael Sweeney (his *Unsung Masters*, screened recently on Channel Five, I saw from the TV listings someone had described as a landmark). His opening remarks were a sweeping survey of Egon Schiele, to whom Marisa was compared. I have that catalogue still, as is the case with many such mementoes dating from that era in my life:

> Egon Schiele (1890–1918) was an Expression-
> ist painter, draftsman, and printmaker, who

achieved notoriety with the erotic nature of much of his figurative work. No genuine art is ever pornographic, we might rather say now. While a student at the Vienna Academy – from 1907 to 1909 – he was greatly influenced by the German Art Nouveau. He met Gustav Klimt, who led the Vienna Sezession group, and absorbed something of Klimt's decorative grace into the line of his own work. Yet unlike Klimt, Schiele's emphasis was more on expression, less on decor, with the power of his line feverish almost. Right from the start he dealt with the human figure, with precisely that erotic candour only certain ladies of the shires worry much about today. Important among Schiele's output are *The Self Seer* (1911), *The Cardinal and Nun* (1912), and *Embrace* (1917), the influence of which you can see in the present exhibition...

Illuminating perhaps, yet I knew nothing of either Schiele or Klimt, and so made a mental note to correct that deficiency – a good library somewhere, or a trawl through encyclopaedias. Meanwhile that pugilistic little man in his suit still hadn't given up on his discounts, and now that I heard – as Marisa answered him again – a definite strain in her voice, I decided to intervene.

'Actually those two pieces have been withdrawn from

sale,' I said. 'As have all these remaining.'

'I see. And who might you be?' The flesh of his large square face tested all the angry shades I knew, from yolk to a burnt orange, to a deeply meaning puce.

'This young lady's agent. Moreover hotfoot from the art markets in New York. We've got a deal, Marisa. All these I'm shipping across the pond tomorrow. Pardon my jetlag.'

Marisa, as jagged as those lines she spirited into being under all that rapid brushwork, stood there foggy in her silence, and remained so until her tormentor had to give her up – a stumpy little man boldly marching out.

'Well, thanks.'

'That's okay, but I mean it. You should withdraw this stuff.'

'You weren't really in New York.'

'Er, no.'

'Ah, well, I know what you're going to say: it's derivative.' For therein lay all Marisa's easy talents.

'That I wouldn't know – though perhaps Michael Sweeney's telling me it is. But that's not it.'

I added, a little recklessly, that every thousand she managed to make here, I'd turn into five. 'You'll get nowhere like this…'

The island of Marisa's artistic youth, only hours ago caressed by pacific waves, she backward glanced, looking helpless as it started to recede. Soon we'd see it gone, with

100

all its tropical sunset, that huge fiery globe cooled under a distant horizon, where already a softer light turned her fantasy of palms to silhouettes, and her golden sands to shadows. There was no resisting the Mephistophelic price I put on her soul, for at last I'd succeed in my aims, filtering all her endeavours through the cold northern dawns native to my territory, my razor mind dulled by musty ledgers, and that acquaintance I had with tax computation tables, and the drouth in my heart as I studied her VAT returns. I detected the same pout and sense of moral outrage as when I'd urged her not to sell her inheritance, and on the proceeds backpack round the world for half her life. Yet she agreed – under the same duress (my common sense), and with the same misgivings, and with all that artistic bile that she and her daddy so easily summoned – agreed unconditionally to close off the Bayswater operation, right here, right now, and hand the whole management issue to me, *meo periculo*.

'If I don't sell these paintings I'll buy them myself.'

Bruce Senior, all through his latter years, lavished hours on the purely mercantile inherent in his friendships, and troubled himself enormously with the Tory office, Kensington, where he knew its constituency activists. I was well placed for a few choice phone calls, and once more had heaped in my ear sincere commiserations, and heard again how terrible a time this was for my mother and me. All that etiquette over with, I cut to the business, and in only a few hours had a deal in principle, exchanging the gallery in Bayswater for something more prestigious at the heart of the wealth in Kensington. I re-priced Marisa's artefacts accordingly, and asked Michael Sweeney for a lengthier disquisition, one that placed her in a definite tradition, rather than hint that she might be a hanger-on. The catalogue I had revamped, and got someone at the office to mail it out to all I knew with bottomless pockets, three or four days before the final launch. The whole exercise proved a success, with the minor stash I made re-invested via a process you'd these days have to call insider trading. The harvest that reaped I presented to Marisa, finally – in the form of a very robust-looking cheque, my commission having already been deducted.

Haphazardly crossing in the post was an invitation to one further spurt in Marisa's recent initiatives, a shapeless splurge for theatre she'd devised with a group of others – under the feminist banner, of course – and one they'd managed to place in a festival out on the fringe. The venue was the Warehouse Theatre, Croydon, which I was just about willing to drive to. I tempered the occasion with a hearty proletarian dinner in one of those tarty bistros so fashionable at that time – a burger in a bun besmeared in griddled Stilton, a golden heap of fries, and a ladle of garlic mushroom arranged as the flattish lowland to that very unholy mountain. As a starter I had a green salad, sluiced with English ale.

I felt I knew roughly what to expect from that tiny theatre incongruously defiant at all that urban concrete abloom in the thoroughfares of Croydon (here is a tip: never visit the Whitgift Centre in the days preceding Christmas). The whole Western world it seemed disparaged its own shaky strides into a future awash with money and opportunity, a state of things that men like me were meant to be highly remorseful of. It was always a credit to the sense of irony Marisa and her ilk encountered in me that all their flirtatious pressure groups – I mean the whole gamut, or on nights like this the harlequinade – would find me as jaded by their cause as the cause was disgusted at the world. The problem with those at the spearhead of change – at least in an age of celebrity – was that the transaction they entered into was as Mephistophelean as that cheque in the post ensnaring my own Marisa (in the end everything *is* a transaction). The obstacle for all the have-nots is how bad they are at business. Business is commerce, and commerce is human exchange. What ya got then mate? What ya got fer me to buy?

To the Marisa of that time anyone who did not share her opinions was necessarily a fascist. This did not prevent me agreeing wholeheartedly with *The Guardian* review her Warehouse piece merited the following day – a cutting I keep with all my other things preserving my faithful thoughts for her.

ETA, or *Estimated Time of Arrival*, is the Bezzazz Theatre Co production that swept all before it at the Warehouse festival last night.

At its most direct, this hour-long play is about the problems of eating disorders, debated and dramatised through three adult sisters – Alexis, Beth and Jocasta – brought together to celebrate the first anniversary of Jocasta's divorce. At this point the problem seems to be all hers. She's a compulsive eater, which we learn of through her opening monologue, against film footage showing her latest frenzy of supermarket shopping. Not surprisingly, the condition she wrestles with she must keep private and secret, with the burden she bears veiled from public display, her life torn to tatters once it's become an endless meal binge.

Alexis and Beth are, by contrast to her, slim and sylph-like, and much more attuned to our media paradigms of 'perfect' womanhood. But *they* have their problems too. Alexis is a high-flyer in the cosmetics industry, and therefore must hold to the view that culture isn't culture unless it's youth culture. She of course will age like the rest of us, a process that no anti-wrinkle cream will ever truly reverse. The third sister, Beth, is clinically ill-disposed to the material invasiveness packaged in all our mass markets, and, obsessive about what may and may not enter her body, does everything she can to keep at bay the chemical infiltrations routine to our food industries. She does this sometimes to the point of anorexia.

It is something that Beth herself utters that binds the whole assured performance to a deeper psychological meaning, when she describes her condition as 'starving for love.' For are we in danger that the acutely felt consciousness of self-image – how as individuals we appear to the world, and not taken as we are – is on the brink of a kind of group neurosis, driven by the media and propagandised into consumerism?

The play is fast-paced, and presented as 'bar-room' Punk, using a wide range of photo imagery against an original soundtrack. It is directed by Marisa Rae, with the three sisters played by Rae herself, Eleanor Prunt and Deborah Beade.

Where are those other two now? And which part did Marisa play?

19

FOR SOMEONE SO strikingly well adapted to the mere surface requirements of formularised hospitality, Henrietta – my good, conventional wife – is for me, and after all these years, still too often disarming in remembering the things I have said. One little triumph we share is her annual garden party, the prime entry on so many calendars hanging from kitchen doors throughout the English shires. The whole spectrum of high and low society has peppered our guest list over the years, from an American man of letters, to a distant Norwegian royal. From our own shores there was even, once, a prime minister in waiting. Further down the scale – though not much, I suspect – was one of those hapless Tories, caught with his hands to a brown-paper parcel full of fivers, a man thereafter forced into one of those hopeless media openings (often with his painted wife in tow), pronouncing on English jurisprudence wherever its 'perverse' judgements manifested themselves.

Habitually I have the laptop open on the breakfast-room table as I eat my morning egg, and with each delicious scoop declaim to myself my diary for the day. The name Lester Gravitt has cropped up once or twice just lately, though I'm vigilant in never voicing that sacred amphibrach, Marisa. That doesn't seem to have stopped a whole history of recent Henriettas glancing at the screen – ostensibly to and fro between here and the hob, or delving in the oven for its lightly heated rolls. This morning the name Gravitt she was mildly scathing about, because of its association with 'the Rae woman.'

'No worries there,' I said. 'That was all years ago.'

Later, when the man himself rose to the dizzy heights of my office suite, he had more than ever that verminous look, and a certain joyful malice in his eye. In a brief if oceanic wave of paranoia, I could even suspect he'd calculated all too accurately my real interest in 'the Rae woman,' and had somehow passed this information to my wife. Absurd, of course – so do snap out of it. I asked him to report his state of progress, which involved yet another catalogue of failure. His most promising client to date, a sudsy individual who'd said his money was in betting (it turned out he'd owned a stud farm) had suddenly sold up and left for the South Pacific. Some of Gravitt's other prospects had had to admit they'd got no money at all.

'Okay. You had any further luck with this Marisa – what was it? – Rae...?'

'Rae, yes.'

It seemed he had of sorts. Her daughter Alicia had

received him in a hotel lounge somewhere in Hertfordshire, not far from a Hollywood wedding scene that — when the weather was right — was due to be shot. The movie it belonged to was one of those schmaltzy anodyne middle-American confections supposedly to do with *our* middle-Englishness. It's the sort of thing I never watch (without a crossword in my lap), but Henrietta does. Poor Lester was kept waiting nursing endless cappuccinos, until finally Alicia retreated to the lift and returned once more with her mother.

Together they strode across the hotel lounge, a slab of England armies of domestic staff had turned to antiseptic, and littered all over with wicker furniture and a jungle of potted flora. The two women were siblings surely — same height, same slim figure, the same dignified deportment. Well, no, not quite — yet that was evident only when he rose from his table, and shook Marisa's hand. All was merely a part of her illusion — that old technique not entirely unknown to her. The years of hard business decisions had set her eyes and the shape of her mouth into a cold, stony fixation, at least when she listened and did not speak. A very faint pencil line above her upper lip bespoke the maturity her daughter did not have. What *she* had was nubility. Nor was Marisa at all flummoxed by Lester's market vocabulary, seeming to know the ins and outs of the products he'd got on offer. She'd got and had studied his portfolio, and had ringed in red ink the ones she was pleased for him to talk about.

'Some of our clients, yes, I'm sure would take a look at these.'

Gravitt stuttered out something about the kind of commission she might expect, but there she cut him short.

'This is not the right moment,' she said.

Alicia signalled a waiter and ordered a freshly squeezed orange whizzed in crushed ice. Gravitt had another cup of cap. Marisa parted with her room number.

'Did she talk very much about her clients?' I asked.

Lester, when it was clear she wouldn't be signing up for anything today, did guide his polite little chit-chat off in that direction. That wedding scene I mentioned had at its centre the most exciting entry in her lists, a boyish Thesp with tousled hair and a meek, if winning smile. Today, if that drizzle ever cleared, saw the moment when all of English society gathered at the altar, just when the movie's many-scripted malcontent declared an impediment. Very pointed comedy. Tra-la.

'Did Ms Rae ever mention my name at all?' I probed.

'Why on earth should she?'

'What I meant, did she mention the company name, in the same breath say as any of our rivals?'

Talk of rivals prompted Gravitt to his *coup de grâce*, now that he'd come to view this glittering opportunity I'd handed him – a chance to carve his own niche in one of those floors below me – as nothing other than a line in door-to-door sales. He'd used his time more wisely than this, applying for alternatives and attending half a dozen interviews. Here, formally, was one month's notice.

Naturally I called on George, our security chief, who supervised Gravitt in clearing his desk, and with suitable gravity escorted him off the premises. I had my back to the window as – a tiny speck on the windy pavement below – he trotted off for an early lunch. Deeply I contemplated one of those pictures on my office wall, signed Marisa Rae, which Gravitt had passed and ignored a dozen times perhaps. Here were those jagged, distorted lines, all that crude brushwork, colours that jarred, the whole charged with atmosphere, and young emotions of that time. Was it all for her career, or was it really frustration, disgust, a deep discontent at the ugliness, the banality, the unutterable paucity of contemporary life?

I remained now as then small in sympathy for the social agenda – all that arty agitprop – that had informed her public works, knowing as I did that those at the top of her league, having now risen to further pre-eminence, wielded a disproportionate influence on our life and our little nutshell world. You could see them almost nightly on our screens, their one purpose to sap our might, their weapon a monotonous reiteration of what is the most dilute or narrow in the making of opinions.

But then Gravitt would never know.

110

20

I COULDN'T MUCH desist from certain jaded observations, making my way, as arranged, through the green room, Croydon, a dingy ill-lit interior as it rapidly filled with people and tobacco smoke. I couldn't for the moment see Marisa, or either of her partners, Eleanor Prunt or Deborah Beade. I stood at the bar and gazed round blankly at the walls, their dark textured paper hung with photographic scenes from past productions. The whole stage range in fact, from a deboshed Roman emperor, tasting death at the hands of a tired praetorian guard, to a man in only his Y-fronts, ironing a shirt in the chaos of his bedsit.

Presently Marisa did appear, in a new guise again and adapted well to the bizarre social mores native to Drury Lane – huge hugs and big hellos for people one barely knew. Her most fervent embrace was for a newspaperman, or critic (or so he was later introduced to me, over a reluctant handshake), the moment, I'd guess, her small theatrical triumph was destined for his plaudits in the morning press. Amazingly she showed the same affection for me, even brushing my cheek with the warmth of her lips. For the Marisa I'd known thus far this was almost unheard of. There was nothing in our worldly lives — no touch of the hand, no arm in arm — that ever betrayed that fury of our lovemaking, that union so lovelessly voyaged after under the eaves of Aitkin Aspires.

Her hack from *The Guardian* left us, that review (which I have kept) no doubt forming its first fragmented sentences as he strode for his bus, train or taxi. We sat at a small round table, its surface a patina of wax, charred at odd points round its perimeter with cigarette burns. Mine was one of the many utility chairs, upholstered in a dirty if durable cherry-coloured plastic. El and Deb descended on us there (more of those hugs, with extravagant salutations), and drank the first of their two Pernods apiece. I had a gin, and drowned it in tonic.

I cannot now remember the course of our conversation, and recall only how unnaturally slim — even more so than Marisa — the two of them were, their shoulders pointed and bony, and facially the structure of each girl's profile almost skeletally defined. To my astonishment again, Marisa touched and caressed my hand, this time doing me the honour of explaining exactly why. Such largesse she had always known me for had reached its zenith in the cheque I had sent, which I hadn't expected to arrive so soon. It meant her publicity project could now get properly underway, with all the costings that entailed.

112

The product of all my *denarii* I saw samples of some weeks later, as she unpacked them from a box she'd heaved to her kitchen table. By this time the bulk had already been distributed to the arts organisations in London and the suburbs where the thing was on sale, a pamphlet – well produced, from what I could see of the cover.

'Hands off!' she said. 'These are review copies.' I'd be getting mine later, after she'd counted them out.

I couldn't quite bring myself to the high-pitched journalese in the glossy women's weeklies her photo and 'extraordinary' story appeared in, or could find opportunity for the daytime radio the purr of her interview voice cascaded over the airwaves from. Yet the story did of course reach me in the end: how on a routine photo session not long ago in New York she had sought out, in one of those dirty, deserted, cobbled back streets, a hardcore pornographer she'd heard about; how she had posed for a whole cameraful of shots, her every conceivable orifice filled or probed by the five robust and rather gormless-looking men picked out for the job. As payment she'd negotiated all rights to half a dozen of the negatives, using one of them here, uncensored – no black ingots inking out offending genitalia – the explicit nature of which she'd constructed her sexual thesis on. This when I read it added nothing to current debates.

She did not solicit my views, but I offered them anyway. 'I'm very disappointed,' I said.

113

She scoffed. 'Don't be such a reactionary.'

'I'm not – and I don't think *you're* a radical.'

'What's that supposed to mean?'

'You're saying what everyone's saying. It's an opportunity wasted.'

'Don't you really mean it's money wasted – your money? Don't worry about that, Bruce. Every penny I owe you, it'll all be paid back.'

'It's not cash I've lost – it's you.'

'All money's dirt money.'

So our rather pointless argument went on, she insisting that the disgusting strictures of capitalism led us all into errors of some sort, while all I could say was the world was complex. Something had to represent our human commerce, and at this stage in our evolution money was it, the lifeblood of all our activities.

'No, Bruce. It's an act of appropriation.'

'Its no more an act of appropriation than a crafted public image is, which you seem so good at just now.'

'You would say that, Bruce.'

How couldn't I? After all, I could not help hold to the view that it must be in the interests of publicly profiled activists to blur the distinction between their careers and their radicalism, involving the same artifice I'd found in Marisa's publication. Here all she asked was a well-worn question: was this the exploitation of women by men, or was it the exploitation of men with cash or credit cards by media corporations, where women were merely chattels? And which of those was more demeaning? Or was it more deeply defiled than that, and here was no more than the scandal she sought in launching her career? I said as much, and was interdicted again, a man more cynical than even she had thought.

Whether or not I had a point, far from project her into the stratosphere of feminist iconography, she found herself inundated instead with correspondence from many kinds of different women, all saying they 'identified' with her. What they wanted to know was how, in a male-encrusted world, their own talents stood to be recognised. Some asked if this was going to be a regular publication, and if so would she consider their enclosures for the next issue – tales of arranged marriages, foot-binding, irksome religious observances, female circumcision, incest, child abuse, and quite a lot of other awful things besides.

The flood of mail went on for days, all of which she vaguely considered incinerating. In the end she replied to the twenty or thirty I picked for her at random, but she tired of this in the heat of the afternoon. I followed her glance through her kitchen window, where both of us caught the gleam from her petrol cap, her bike denuded of its rain sheet and awaiting minor repairs.

That was it, she must have thought. The idea of Spain had beckoned again.

21

HOME FOR ME now is a grey, sombre mansion, its severe if self-effacing grandeur enfolded in the rolling hills of England, somewhere in a remote valley in Berkshire. Here Henrietta lives her simple socialitic life, while for me, after the day's weary work, I enjoy my simple domestic leisure. I found the place by accident, on the first Saturday after I'd announced my engagement to Henrietta. Friends of her family had invited us both to a house party – not here, but far across the hills at a neighbouring address. I had noted down the details hastily on my pad at work, but once I'd got it in my car I winced at the pencilled map I'd attempted to draw. It started mid-page with the road and roundabouts taken off the motorway, and ended in a squish in one corner for the most vital signs and turn-offs.

A first finger of dusk found me driving up- and downhill along a narrow, unmade track, where all around me the trees, shrubs and hoary old men were silhouetted on the peaks, as the sun sank beneath them. Some part of me dreamed on distantly in just that quality of light, but then I got stuck atrociously behind a tractor, an obstacle that didn't move aside for several miles. By then I was mesmerised, and for sheer monotony laboured well beyond my turn (metronomic, the back of the driver's shaven head, as it bobbed up and down). I'd awaited a sign that never came, and of course eventually found the wrong lane, more hopeful than convinced this had to be it.

I should have had my suspicions when more than once I had to stop the car and open a gate, or slow for a cattle grid. Then I thought it odd that a gent in a waxed country jacket, the shotgun he carried pointing at a tuft of grass, should regard me so balefully, distant though he was. Meekly I smiled and waved and drove to the house, where the track had given way to a vast macadam drive. Here the truth prevailed, when the only two cars I could see were a shiny vintage Daimler, and alongside it a dusty Morris Minor. Depressingly the whole house front was unlit at the windows. Nor could I detect, even faintly, any slight sound carried on the night air resembling party chatter. Only a muffled farm machine droned. I parked up and approached the forbidding oaken door. I pulled the bell chain. The small boy who answered wasn't quite as I'd anticipated, a sleepy look in his eye, and a thumb that went to his mouth so soon as I spoke.

The young woman who came out after him – not his mother, but a nanny or helper – told me what I'd already deduced – that I'd got the wrong house. I looked at her blankly, a man unstarred without maps or road signs – but did presently comprehend her very detailed directions. These, intermittently gestured by first *her* hand then mine, took me where I couldn't see, over the brow of a hill.

To get there took another twenty minutes or so, though there were no mishaps this time. A line of parked cars snaked from the drive and into a paddock, into which I added mine. The chink of glasses and a tinkle of merry conversation chimed in the night air. Then the house as I approached could not have contrasted more with the ancient grey façade, and the symmetric crenellations, I had just left behind. It belonged with cocktails, its bald architectural lines a flat roof and curved corners, with lots of white paint edged in lime green. The windows were large and unadorned, with metal frames, while a reddish golden powdery light gently spilt out through their crystal.

I drank a Martini, followed by bottled water, followed by another Martini. Henrietta was radiant and sparkling, of course, and when we danced there was genuine intimacy. Late in the evening she introduced me to our host, to whom I related the flaws in my recent itinerary. I told him how much I admired that first house I'd called at, its solid medieval gloom just that kind of cocoon a man who dealt in the frenetic world of business every day might wish to retire to when he came home late at night.

'Might soon have your chance,' he said.

'Oh?'

'Place belongs to Lord Etoll, who's had to sell off the

family silver. Rumour has it the house'll be next. Oh and by the way congratulations.' He beheld me smilingly, then planted a gentle kiss on Henrietta's cheek.

The evening passed in a whirl of further inconsequentialities, and for me ended shortly after twelve — Henrietta's pumpkin hour — when (with both her glass slippers intact) I escorted her out to the car that had called for her. No guilt at all did I feel when, seated and ready to go, her large hazel eyes fixed on me — innocent and expectant. I said some late business had emerged, which would keep me in Spain for the next week or ten days, or thereabouts.

'A property deal,' I explained.

'Well — have a good flight, and send me a postcard. Phone.'

I drove home, the radio a dead blind hum in its cotton-wool wrap — some unearthly late discussion show. In the morning I called on Marisa, and found her at her kitchen table, her spirits slightly dulled under the leaden waves and the weight of her accumulating mail sacks. With what little nonchalance the situation allowed, she was breakfasting on soft cheese and celery. Down there outside below us a mechanic tinkered with her bike.

'Bedroll all packed up?' I asked. 'Ready to go?'

'You bet.'

I got her to show me on the map the route she intended to take, and in the morning, bright and early in the office,

I booked a flight for myself and arranged my hire car. I called on Marisa again and gave her a long list of places – with dates and times I'd worked out meticulously – where we might meet. A café I knew in Carcassonne she said no to. A good fish restaurant I had visited in Barcelona was slightly more *propicio*. I could recall, too, a public garden in València, where as a very small boy I had picked up and smoked a discarded *cigarello*.

'And Cádiz I love, and the north bank of the Guadalete.'

No, she said: 'No bebo jerez. And anyway, can you afford to take time off?'

'I've got contacts. I'll rustle up some foreign business.'

That side of things – the business – was never as problematic as things to do with Marisa. It was only with her that nothing was ever clear-cut. Of the many dates and addresses I gave her, she managed only three, and with one of those had a man in tow. He I had nothing against, a young, curly-haired Dutch boy, learning to paint the hard blue brightness of cloudless southern skies (whether under Marisa's tutelage I didn't ask).

On the last of these rendezvous she was an hour late almost, but mercifully alone. I had wound my way up the hilly stretch of road to the peak of the Alhambra plateau, and there waited in the spacious coach park outside its Moorish palace. I had my tourist guide and a phrasebook, but soon tired of these. All the windows were down, but nevertheless I sweltered in the heat. Soon I'd decamped outside, sprawling on the bonnet, my back to the windscreen, my sunhat cocked forward on my forehead. I woke I don't know how many minutes after that, some ever wakeful part of me having detected the deep purr of Marisa's engine, as at last she'd arrived, ascending slowly up the hill.

The meeting was not a success. She was tired and distracted, and hardly responsive at all – not to *me*, and not to those revamped Moorish splendours. In fact I got not much out of her until La Acequia Courtyard, where the terraced gardens, pools and fountains soothed whatever mental aches she'd got. I asked her what was wrong. She said it was hugely disappointing that all she'd managed to do was run away. I asked her what she meant by that.

She said she had no doubts or qualms concerning what she'd done (meaning the photographs), but the pose was such a commonplace that no one had been shocked. What she'd intended as politically transgressive was viewed as no more than entertainment by those she'd transgressed against.

'How could I get is so wrong?'

'It's too early to say you have got it wrong.'

One other thing she hadn't planned for, and this I told her now, was my preparedness to break off my engagement with Henrietta. In the pool at our feet I watched very carefully as a small ripple I had noticed enlarged itself unexpectedly, a phenomenon precisely

121

synchronised to that one, cool, dispassionate moment she chose to advise me not to abandon my marriage plans.

The following day I flew home, to a cold and wet Heathrow.

22

I WAITED AND watched my mail, but bar a card from Cordova I heard nothing more from Marisa – a ghostly kind of absence that seemed to go on long after the date she'd planned for her return. So far as Henrietta might judge, much good there was, when three of my expats had offered the use of various holiday properties should we wish to honeymoon in Spain. I, personally, wasn't keen, having too many associations – a psychology I kept to myself – wishing only to forget that first decisive sense of loss I now felt about Marisa. Yet perhaps it was only a matter of time before another of her invitations floated onto my doorstep, and I even saw something in the press about other ventures she'd embarked on – though still nothing came. Too much of this I couldn't bear. I broke the deadlock, hand delivering an invitation of my own – an envelope she opened with a smile.

'Congratulations,' she said.

'Why thanks!'

'You've made a good choice.'

'But under duress.'

'Duress, Bruce?'

'It's a tribal thing. Your clan and mine don't mix, and that I regret.'

'You can't choose where you're from.'

'You *can* say where you're going. And anyway there are visas, passports.'

'That's a touch liberal – for you.'

'You think that's out of character?'

The wedding was set for June, but, before that, work was scheduled for Chiswick, with a chimney that had to be relined, and a conservatory that Henrietta wanted built. I brought in some decorators too, and spent whole mornings with my affianced measuring for curtains, which I left it to her to choose (and a good choice she made).

Disappointingly Marisa came to the ceremony only, forgoing the reception afterwards, which was at Henrietta's family home in Bicester. So my fate was sealed, in a small parish church my in-laws had strolled to every Sunday morning for the last quarter century, its yews, its village bell, its lychgate. No one voiced an impediment, for only I knew the truth, looking out from the centre aisle, where at last my eyes roved where the day's heavenly bondings had been at their most intense, Marisa seated in a distant pew. I might have found her easy to miss, half hidden away under the cold shadow of a pillar, or failed to see it was her by the unaccustomed clothes she wore. A short blossom-coloured jacket with matching skirt, had, to complete the triad (chromatically), a soft beret worn at a jaunty little angle. A lip-gloss and a slightly meretricious shading round the eyes were not the kind of makeup I had ever seen her wear. I smiled.

A box I kept in my dormitory at school, with its lock and key to the sacred objects of my life – letters from home, or gifts I'd been given at holiday time – I treat with the same sanctity today, in a desk drawer in one of my private upper rooms (in Berkshire. Lord Etoll's former place). Its contents ceased to be those boyish things decades ago, and were replaced by lifelong monuments to Marisa. Just now I put away again her *ETA* programme, to cover what it had uncovered, that pornographic image of herself – *The Five Phallus Photo*. What I'm looking for is wedding shots, but all I can find involving her are group portraits, in lines three or four deep outside the church porch. I can just about make out that flaming beret, and an insouciant smile. I don't have any that were taken at the reception, because Marisa wasn't there – one of those few decisions she made I saw the wisdom of. Henrietta's father had rigged up his several terraced lawns with voluminous open tents, each with a quartet of dining tables seating eight. Here would Marisa have been, unpartnered, an arts polymath, expected to find (somehow) suitable small talk among bankers and lawyers, insurance people, property developers – the whole business enterprise in fact.

Recently I've added to my box, some few things slave

125

to my scrutiny again, here under a thin autumnal light, my afternoon fading into a less private Sunday night, with Henrietta due back soon across the fields, having taken the dogs. I got them off Gravitt's computer and out of his desk drawers, once I was satisfied George had seen him safely off the premises. Odd objects number a Rae Agency pocket diary, packed at its opening information pages with all sorts of useful web and email addresses, and of course phone numbers too. As I'd expect, documents I pulled off his hard drive aren't much more than working papers, which I glanced only briefly before I burnt them to disc. I also have his entire email history, which makes laborious reading, and cruel false leaps of the heart when I reassemble exchanges between himself and Marisa Rae (marisa@raeagency.com). I see she splutters through many a mistyped word, and dispenses with punctuation. And it's sad because nowhere does she ever betray her once intimate connection with the firm that Gravitt used to work for. A 'Give my regards to Bruce' surely wasn't a lot to ask.

Forms he filled in while hanging off his phone consist mostly of partially edited tables and spreadsheets, keyed I suppose left-handed. One for Marisa reads: Name, Marisa Marti Rae; DOB, blank; POB, Northwick Park Hospital; Marital status, single; Address, 27 Goldhurst Terrace, NW6; Nationality, etc. One for Alicia is almost identical – Alicia Marsi Rae, nativity Toulouse.

However, time to put this stuff away, and turn the computer off. Here comes Henrietta, five golden retrievers yapping at her heels. Time for me get downstairs and stroll through the wine cellar. It's steaks tonight, I think.

23

I TRIED AS a matter of policy, throughout our first year of married life, to ensure as full a social calendar as the demands of work and family allowed. I took particular care that our Chiswick weekends were vibrant with party chatter, according to time of year. Pigs, lambs, chickens all fell prey to my open spits, once we had reached that dizziest height of the barbecue season (*une saison en enfer*). Come the first equinox (the autumnal one – not forgetting H and I had wed in June) our very gentle guests were led through the ensilvered snares of our garden, and in a potion of shadows saw the magnum I had brought popped and poured. There under a harvest moon all raised glasses in expectation of fuller granaries to come. November was bonfires, and fireworks, and *Beaujolais nouveau*. Christmas saw Henrietta's birthday, and a charged glass held unabashed to the fullest light of the world. As ever our new year was a prosperous one, and shared with all our friends. Now usher in, please, equinox number two (vernal, by this reckoning), when a score or more of us drank a druidic peace from tankards of ale. April's sweet zephyrs blew in acts of pilgrimage (*my* birthday this time, and another new tax year), friends bearing gifts, and hearty at my table, feasting on a home-cooked roast.

The one thing wrong was Marisa, who in every case secretly headed my guest list, yet consistently failed to arrive. Sometimes she replied to my invitations, to let me know that this would be the case. More often I heard and saw nothing. Come June, and my first anniversary, I tried to suggest that I wasn't bothered at all if Marisa had found someone. Whoever that might be, he was welcome too – in fact I'd be very pleased to meet. I think it pained me more that this was not her obstacle.

Bruce Three was born on a frosty November night, a long if uncomplicated process, dulled in my own recollections by the problems *I* met, an anxious man apace in a spotless maternity suite, looking for something to read. The absence of anything honed my preference to surfaces only – prurient tabloids, or society mags, or even teenage weeklies. These latter I could chortle over then, if not in later years (don't you ever read these, Three. These are for morally horrified fathers only, always alert to the corruptibility of youth). For several hours I jangled my pockets for change, magnetised into the plasticised light of the coffee machine, a monstrous presence always looming in the corridor, and very specific as to the coinage it would take.

A litter of polystyrene beakers attested to my

wakefulness when, finally, my presence was required – for only I should dab damp flannels to Henrietta's burning brow. But, eventually, Bruce Three was a bonny babe, tipping the scales at a customary seven pounds something. I allowed myself to be told, in all the worldly nonchalance a man can muster, that Henrietta required a stitch or two – a procedure, with all its attendant conversation, I preferred not to watch. I drove home, very slightly shattered, and under the anaesthesia that came in a brandy bottle snoozed in my living room till dawn. The following day I returned with flowers and toiletries, and a mental list of prospective godparents. Marisa was my first choice, of course, and – perhaps reminded of her pledge – she did accept that office, very promptly on the phone, and in a loud bouquet of smiles.

'A boy, wonderful! Got a name yet?'

'Bruce Three.'

'Three eh? Not the third, or one one one?'

'Bruce Three.'

The christening took place on a cold, dry, sunny January morning, for which Marisa wore a provocative outfit, its shade a blazing super-nova. Photographs I have. In the one I keep in my box she's got the infant in his swaddling, held to her shoulder and patted on the back – a scene I remember, a husband also frozen in his pose, a champagne flute halted suddenly and nowhere near my lips, the thought in my head an almost permanent regret as to the boy's maternity. For his christening present she'd bought a job lot of brightly coloured toys that hung on his cot, and rattled when touched or moved. Beyond that she never acknowledged birthdays, or wrote with friendly advice as to how to be a good Christian, or capitalist, or whatever she thought we wanted him to be. I tried to take this up with her only a few days after Three was one, and with slight trepidation dialled her number. I got through almost immediately, only to be told, by the tenant now manning her phone, that Marisa had delayed her tertiary education long enough, she felt, and had enrolled for a philosophy degree at the University of Kent.

I phoned that institution, and got no further than its admin block, where a slightly distant female, whose age I couldn't determine, gave me an address where first-year students generally picked up their mail. Naturally I wrote. The reply was a phone call at the office a week to ten days later, when the principle seemed less important, and I was more interested in why she had chosen philosophy.

'Well, one needs a degree,' she said.

'Yes, but why philosophy?'

'Oh, that's easy. I've always had sympathies with Wittgenstein.'

'Well thanks for the tip – I'll look him up. Don't suppose you'd like to meet?'

'I'm free tomorrow evening.'

The best I could negotiate was a drive to the pub she

131

named, a long laboured trawl up and down those Kentish hills, the end to which was an accidental stumbling on the place, though when I'd sat there an hour I had reason to doubt both my sanity and the venue. This *was* The Golding Hop, I assumed. Why yes, with its blacked beams, beaten copper platters, and a charred green log fizzing in the grate. I nursed my pint for another ten minutes, then, on the point of quaffing the whole thing down, Marisa, miraculously, arrived. She was pale, distant, not at all communicative, and unusually for her wore a long skirt, boots with heels, a very heavy cardigan. Her drink was also new – a Jim Beam – which she sipped at sparingly, declining a second when I offered. She asked politely after the family, to which I answered perfunctorily. 'Growing and glowing,' I think I must have said. I asked what was wrong. Medically, she said, the diagnosis was a lack of iron in her diet, and this explained her listlessness. 'Eat plenty of liver,' I advised. The suggestion didn't appeal. I fingered my car keys, knowing, and overwhelmingly subdued, that I'd lost her forever, though couldn't have believed that this was the last time I'd see her. Now of course I have the benefit of hindsight, and Gravitt's documentation, and the certainty from Alicia's date of birth that Marisa was several months pregnant. It seems so poignant – how I could have sat there, hopelessly looking at my fob watch, having to contemplate the long ride home.

I saw her out to her car, a 2CV she had parked nearer

to the exit than mine. She sat at her wheel and spoke through the window, all with such lassitude I couldn't bear to take any more of her precious time. 'Goodbye,' I said, 'goodbye.' I sat in my own car and watched for the pulse of exhaust from hers. Lights flicked on. Then, very deliberately, she swung round and out in the Kentish lanes. I inserted the key and turned my engine on, but by now I'd lost her — gone to the nothings of my night.

24

IN ONE OF his rare moments of paternal warmth, Bruce Senior once explained to me that all marriages from royalty down were a negotiated settlement, where success did not depend on the vagaries, or the uncertainty of love. Good partnerships ran along much the same lines in business and in matrimony. Perhaps subconsciously I adhered to that good principle, in the leisure and latitude I wreathed round Henrietta's life, so long as I – that eternally guilty male – remained aloof from the chores and disciplines childrearing brings. On the other hand, had my union been with Marisa – or should I say an equal partnership – that gifted being would have made me broker something other, and break with family tradition. As it was, as Bruce Three grew older, a little spoilt, and certainly more demanding, I spent correspondingly more time away from the hearth, the pretext always understood – that the business didn't run itself, and the more complex it was the harder I had to work. She had an *au pair* – sometimes she had two – and a domestic team, and other young mothers round her.

On rare occasions when I did come home, I could expect them all here, or a few doors down the street, with tea, coffee or cocktails, partying late in the afternoon. Later, with the boy away at school, she shopped a lot. Whatever her diversion, not much of it mattered to me, a man who nurtured his absence, content to enter his house when only the porch light remained on, a smile and a glaze in his eye, and a surreptitious stench of liquor on his breath.

When Bruce Three was eight – which meant I hadn't seen Marisa for nearly seven years – I was unable to spend the hour or two I'd planned in the West End, looking for the gift I'd intended to buy. I had dismissed, at first, the slight pangs that came with my office mail and morning cups of tea – a dull distant ache I diagnosed as neuralgia. By lunchtime its full fire, whatever it was, inflamed my whole jaw, which resulted, after a trip to my dentist, in the surgical removal of all my wisdom teeth. This, despite the golden credit cards I paid him with, was not an operation he was willing to perform himself, though he did recommend a very good private hospital. There I convalesced, numbed and almost speechless, too distracted to read a book, and too often forced into the arms of idiotic daytime television.

I distinctly remember one afternoon in the day room, with its loud, gigantic television set. This when I first sat down was doling out its discourse to no one in particular –

just someone in the box seat, he in an impatient liaison with all its channels, followed by the kind of consensus, from all those grouped around him, that no one ever voices. I cradled my chin and settled down uncomplainingly, after a nodded hello to the three or four other post-ops already seated.

I was amazed initially, maudlin next, when gradually it became clear that the film being screened was the subject of Richard Adlam's after-dinner speech, at a private house in Denham, all those years ago. Here for me alone, one of Ealing's great filmic moments – and how well I recalled great Ealing moments of my own – was the terror-stricken face of a hapless victim of *something*, crashing through the patio doors, and sprawling on the hard stone floor. A part of me wished to blurt out that I'd seen it all before, though the thought of all the pained sentences that would entail pressed me back in my chair, massaging my jaw.

When I returned home I found that, in my absence, Henrietta had had our bedroom redecorated, and where I had hung two of Marisa's self-portraits there was now a pair of Sisley reprints. She suggested I remove them to the office, where they might be better placed with my other original Raes. That for many reasons I didn't wish to do, and so for several years they remained in a lumber room, sheathed in corrugated paper, and later bubble wrap. It wasn't until our move from Chiswick to Berkshire, where I staked a claim to my own private suite of upper rooms, that I was able to re-hang them. Furthermore, with advances in digital technology, I have had them scanned, and using the printing firm that produces my office stationery I have developed them into postcards. On one of them I wrote,

> Marisa,
>
> As you may know, Lester Gravitt recently tendered his resignation, and therefore is unable to take your portfolio further. In the circumstances I shall be very happy to take charge of your account personally.
>
> Best wishes, Bruce

A stamp I did apply, though trashed the whole thing in the bin. It solved nothing, for still I couldn't let it pass, and in the morning, rather than drive to my local station, I carried on into west London, parking unobtrusively at Ealing Common, in sight of the Rae Agency. Shortly after nine mother and daughter arrived, in a black, metallic four-wheel drive. Marisa stepped out first, as young and slim and lithe as I'd known her twenty-five years ago. She glanced at where I was parked, but didn't catch my eye. Alicia followed her out, then immediately clambered back, in pursuit of something still on the dashboard. My hand hovered on the handle of my door, retracted itself, hovered again, then, in a sudden impulse, swept for the keys, which I fumbled. I restarted the engine. I reversed out, without looking back. Then, in a screech of tyres and a dreamy signal left, I set off again, for the long deserted road back into the sleepy fields of Berkshire.

'No work today, honey?'

'No, not today. Not feeling so good.'